TIME DOESN'T HEAL ALL WOUNDS... ...someTIMES IT TAKES something MORE

Other Books by Wes Funk

Dead Rock Stars (first edition)
Baggage
Cherry Blossoms
Wes Side Story

www.wesfunk.ca

Rock n Roll
Ku-T-t-y

Keep on
truckin
Wes

ILLUSTRATED EDITION

DEAD
ROCK
STARS

WES
FUNK

FOREWORD BY
JAY SEMKO

ART BY KEVIN HASTINGS

yowp
YOUR NICKEL'S WORTH PUBLISHING

DEAD ROCK STARS *(Illustrated Edition)*
Story © 2008 Wes Funk; artwork © 2015 Kevin Hastings; with foreword by Jay Semko
All rights reserved.

Published by Your Nickel's Worth Publishing

Library and Archives Canada Cataloguing in Publication

Funk, Wes, author
    Dead rock stars / Wes Funk ; [illustrated by] Kevin Hastings. — Illustrated edition.

Originally published by Backroads Press, 2011.
ISBN 978-1-927756-41-6 (pbk.)

    I. Hastings, Kevin, 1976-, illustrator II. Title.

PS8611.U66D42 2015   C813'.6   C2015-900654-6

Production made possible with the support of Creative Saskatchewan.

Cover design by Chris Fischer
Book design by Heather Nickel
Artwork photography by Christina Langman and Sevenstar Studio, Saskatoon.
Author/Illustrator photo by Xander Richards

Printed in Canada
www.wesfunk.ca

creative
SASKATCHEWAN

YOUR NICKEL'S WORTH PUBLISHING
REGINA, SK. WWW.YNWP.CA

For all the creative types in Saskatchewan
—we're all in this together.

"I guess we're all gonna be what we're gonna be,
so what do you do with good ol' boys like me?"

– Don Williams

FOREWORD

LOVING THE MUSIC OF LIFE, with the rock 'n' roll casualty rate high, and the reality of family, life, love, and the prairie winter landscape, I spent a good part of my youth in rural Saskatchewan—always on the outside, with rock music, rock star fantasies, and pure love of the genre—those were my best friends.

We all grow up, in one way or another, whether we want to or not, and no matter how much we leave behind, there's always something that keeps us attached, visible or not. I live here now: it is home, and the passion still burns deep—the family ties pull, push, tighten, release, pluck and strum on the heartstrings and nerve endings.

I love *Dead Rock Stars*; Wes Funk captures so many feelings, places, emotions so perfectly … down-home Saskie, urban and rural, and exclusively on vinyl, exploding with love and rock stars.

JAY SEMKO
The Northern Pikes

I HEARD THE NEWS TODAY, OH BOY

THE DAY BEGAN like any other. The sun shone brightly down on the melting snow of the city, bringing about the promise of rebirth like it always does at that time of year. Customers came into the shop in effervescent moods and seemed to beam too, in their own way. The impending end of winter always did that to the people of Saskatoon.

I was in a good enough mood myself. It was the beginning of another week and there were things that needed to be done, but having had a weekend's worth of rest, I was prepared to face whatever challenges the day might bring.

The record shop was abnormally busy. I had just unlocked the front door and half a dozen people were already browsing. The store needed a good spring cleaning and perhaps in a bit—when the guys came in—I could have one of them begin the labour-intensive tasks of scrubbing the walls and dusting the corners we were forever neglecting. With one of them doing that and the other watching the cash register, I could disappear into my dingy office in the back and start sorting through the huge stack of records someone had dropped off last Friday. I supposed I could have asked Jim and Ray to go through it all over the weekend, and I'm sure they would have done a sufficient job, but truth be told, I enjoyed doing it.

As I waited for the guys to come in and for people to bring their newfound treasures to the front, I sifted through the box of LPs at the front counter. All the usual stuff was there: albums people thought they'd wanted but found they didn't; one-hit wonders and music that once held appeal but no longer did. I smirked to myself. It was highly unlikely there would be anything in this particular box I might want to buy from this particular customer and set out in the store for resale.

But then you never knew. It's like a treasure hunt. Every now and again, you find something. I've seen it often in the many years I've been in this business. There, in a cardboard box of records too trendy for their own good or scratched vinyl that should have been tossed in the garbage long ago, sometimes lay an album that somebody somewhere was just dying to have.

It's a game to me. It's how I make my living too.

Jim sauntered in just in time to start his shift, bringing me a take-out coffee in recompense for his near-lateness. I happily accepted. I guess when you work alongside someone for so many years, you kind of acquire a strange ability to know what the other thinks or wants.

Ray didn't bring anything with him when he came through the door a few moments later, which was fine. Ray wasn't nearly as considerate or even as outgoing as Jim, but I never expected him to be. He slopped wet snow on the black and white tiles when he came in, but it didn't matter. The three of us had a certain chemistry that somehow worked, day in and day out, and who were any of us to tamper with that?

I rang through some purchases while the guys took off their outdoor gear in the tiny staffroom in the back. It was really all quite typical: a young girl with a face full of piercings and a mop of jet-black hair wanted to trade in a few light-hearted boy band CDs for something a little more goth. An aging hippy purchased a psychedelic album that he clearly couldn't wait to get home to play. An uptight woman wearing way too much makeup bought a couple of Enya discs as background music for the dinner party she was planning. She seemed incredibly anxious to get out of the crowded store with its hodgepodge of humanity. I repressed a smile at the way she threw the hood of her soft-pink winter coat over her perfectly curled blond hair and hurried off down the street.

Somewhere in the back, the phone rang.

Jim came out, smoothing his dreadlocks, and said it was for me. Not knowing how long I'd be, I grabbed my coffee and he took my place at the front counter. As I plunked myself down on the swivel chair and picked up the receiver, I got the sudden feeling that something somewhere was amiss. Call it psychic, call it karma, or just call it instinct, somehow I just *knew*.

"Hello?"

"Jacky, is that you?"

"Sure is."

"This is your mother."

"I know."

"I have some bad news."

RAMBLIN' MAN

EVEN THOUGH IT was nearly spring, grey clouds hung listlessly in the sky on the late March afternoon I began the long drive to my parents' farm. No sunshine, no birds chirping, no signs of life surfacing in the cold hard ground under the snow piled in the ditches. Fine, really. Didn't bother me much. Hell, didn't bother me at all. Matched my mood. Though I didn't mind the drive, I wasn't looking forward to arriving at my destination.

Life had never been easy for me in the little prairie town I was raised in. Never had been, never would be. I'd felt like a piece of shit the whole time I lived there. And even though I'm basically a well-adjusted person now, I felt my spirit spiral down to that old familiar feeling of worthlessness. How pathetic. What does that say about my hometown pride and a reunion with my family?

I felt grey, just like the weather.

My name is Jackson Hill; Jack to all my friends in the city. *Jacky* is what a lot of my family calls me. I hate it, being called Jacky. Hate it a lot. You may be asking, why such an unusual name for a farm-boy raised in the middle of nowhere in rural southern Saskatchewan? Well, my parents chose each of our names for a specific reason. My brother Austin was named after the city in Texas. My mom and dad had once spent several days there many years ago, before any of us were born. They'd gone on a road trip through the U.S. for their honeymoon, and their car broke down in Austin. They ended up spending a lot of time there, holed-up in a cheap motel room while they awaited repairs. And, well, you know what happens in cheap motel rooms.

Nine months later my oldest sibling was born. My second oldest brother, Noel, was born a few days before Christmas. That's self-explanatory. Sucks to be him; he got the girly name. Ironic how the big butch guy in the family got the feminine name, while I, the estranged family fag, made out okay name-wise. No real deep meaning to mine, though. Only that Johnny Cash and June Carter were belting out "Jackson" on the radio of my father's '67 Monte Carlo while he drove my mother forty miles to the nearest hospital when she was in labour with me.

It was all fine with me. My parents, Grace and Owen Hill, might have made mistakes, but that wasn't one of them. I like Johnny Cash. Like him a lot. Like him even more now that he's dead. Now that he's a legend, I mean. Now that he's immortal. Some people are strange that way. I am. How we idolize someone after they're gone. Take Elvis, for instance. Society in general is infatuated with him. He was on velvet in the funky coffee shop I'd bought my take-out coffee in before hitting the road. Everywhere you turned, there he was: on framed prints in funky cafés, hanging out with Marilyn and Bogie and the original rebel without a cause himself, Jimmy Dean. On clocks, coffee mugs, even Christmas trees, bumping and grinding to "Jail House Rock." On tacky collectible plates hanging in the cluttered kitchens of sexually suppressed homemakers. We see him forever as one of the world's sex symbols. Not that he wasn't hot, mind you. But had he actually lived into old age and become a frail old man like so many others, I find myself wondering if we would still see him as the king of rock and roll and the ultimate sex god?

And it's not just him. He's just one of many. Buddy Holly was the original. Then came Jim Morrison, Jimi Hendrix, Bob Marley. It's all the same. More recent ones—Freddie Mercury, Kurt Cobain—the list goes on. Horny teenage girls, bored housewives, and eccentric faggots across the world have lain on their beds, listening to music and indulging in lingering fantasies over these anti-heroes and others like them.

Me included. I'm in the club as well. I like dead rock stars too.

I was listening to the radio now. The one in my '79 Volkswagen Rabbit. A muffled, static remake—Counting Crows' cover of Grateful Dead's "Friend of the Devil." Love the song, love it a lot. Both versions. That song has pissed off countless mothers over the decades since it was written, ears popping as they listened to their sons' hi-fis booming behind the closed bedroom door, wondering what was really going on in there. Is he doing his homework like he said he would? Or is he smoking a cigarette, or worse, a joint? Is he masturbating? Is the song leading him down the path of decadence? Is he becoming demented? Or satanic? But if they'd just listen to the song, perhaps they'd find it's really not so bad. Not bad at all; could be much worse. Life could always be worse.

I looked at my watch. Six thirty; making good time. A seven- hour drive on the province's endless double highway. Not much to see, only prairie; bald, empty fields with patches of snow strewn over them. A few trees, not many. In the hours to come there would be oil wells, but it would be dark by then. Hell, it was almost dark now. I'd only left the city at five thirty. I'd worked all day. Eight 'til five. Only stopped at my condo long enough to grab the duffel bag I'd packed the night before, along with my guitar and my dog.

I love Cassie, love her to death. That's my dog. If you don't get the meaning behind this name, I'm sure as hell not gonna explain it to you. All right, I will: Mama Cass. How I love her. Love her voice, love her clothes, love her presence. Love how being very overweight and sort of unattractive didn't deter her one bit from throwing herself out there in front of endless audiences and belting out John Phillips's fabulously hippy lyrics. I turned to Cassie on the passenger seat beside me and sang to her. She arched her beautiful chocolate-brown head toward me and eyed me up, half adoring and half curious.

"Weren't those just the greatest lyrics?" I asked her. She seemed to agree.

Papa John Phillips and Mama Cass Elliot: dead rock stars both.

I caught a glimpse of myself in the rear-view mirror as I turned my attention back to the road. Tired and pale. My complexion is pretty fair, but I looked withdrawn. I guess I'm exhausted. It had been a long week at work plus trying to prepare for the trip to my folks' place. Busy getting things done. Shades of grey tinted my deep red hair, but it actually looked pretty good. I don't mean to brag, but of the three of us brothers, I think I got the nicest shade of red. Well, Austin's is more of a strawberry-blond really. It always made him look old, even when he wasn't. And Noel is the carrot-top, fiery like him. I got a deep shade, an auburn almost. It looks okay with my goatee and mustache. I wear it cropped short. I like it trim and tousled—"messy" is how my mother describes it. But I think it goes good with the piercings in my ears and the glasses with the heavy black frames I wear. Makes me look like me: damaged, yet likeable.

Seven thirty. I was fading fast. The dark-roast coffee, now cold, hadn't had the rejuvenating effect I'd hoped it would. Didn't help that I'd spilled about a quarter of it on myself earlier, trying to balance the cup between my legs while I manoeuvered the tiny car out of the city's late afternoon rush hour. Cassie had been quite agitated then too. She wasn't accustomed to road trips and had bounced all over the vehicle, confused and disoriented. Now my mother would be wanting to do my laundry as soon as she saw me. She would ask why I wore such faded, worn-out jeans and why most of my T-shirts are black. I like black. Long before the whole gothic rage took over society's youth, I loved black. I look good in it. Pastels and white always make me seem dull and faded. Black makes me look better somehow. Feel better too. The man in black, like Johnny Cash.

Five more hours on the road. How was I gonna make it? I wouldn't, simple as that. I had to stop and rest. I'd spend the night in one of the many dreary little hotels in one of the many small towns that lined the highway. Besides, I wasn't prepared yet to face it all. If I kept going, I would arrive at my parents' at such a late hour; midnight or even one. Better to phone Mom now. I'd tell her to go to bed and I'd see her in the morning.

"Yeah, that's best," I said to Cass.

By nine, I had pulled into the mucky gravel parking lot of a reasonably well-maintained small-town hotel in a hamlet called Turn Soil. It was the kind of tattered-looking old building that hardly ever sees the likes of an overnight guest in its rooms. The kind where the proprietors make their living selling off-sale Canadian beer and serving shots to bored, retired farmers and kids faking that they're of age.

"I need a room for one—oh, and a dog," I said to the chubby old man hunched over the desk. I'd thought *I* looked tired; *he* was white as a ghost. Years of working long, exhausting days running his own business had obviously taken their toll. I presumed he lived in the hotel, kids all grown and scattered across the country with lives of their own. Wife's probably in the back watching television or perhaps working in the bar behind him.

I could see it from where I stood; guys in ball caps and denim and flannel, drinking brewskis, having some laughs, looking at their watches, knowing they should get home soon or their old ladies would be pissed off. If they hurried, she'd be only mildly annoyed. They could still get laid if they arrived back at the farm within the hour. Some were shooting pool, some playing video lottery in the dimly-lit room.

"What do you mean, a dog?" he scowled over his bifocals at me.

"Oh, she's a good dog."

"How big is she?" More scowling. He looked out the filthy, mud-stained front window toward my car. Not a whole lot of people skills going on here.

"She's a chocolate lab. But don't worry. She won't do no damage. Won't bark either," I said, not backing down. It was true, Cassie was better behaved than most people.

He handed me a room key. "You got room six," he grunted, "Check-out's 11:00 a.m. sharp."

"I'll be gone long before then," I said, turning to go. "Oh, can a guy order food in your lounge?"

He took off his glasses. "We do burgers and sandwiches. Grilled cheese and such. If ya really want a hearty meal, go to the Chinaman's down the street. But you better hurry. They mostly close at ten, but sometimes nine thirty."

"Thanks," I replied, opening the weathered front door. A cool breeze immediately began filling the room.

"I recommend combination B," he called after me. "Costs a little more, but you get an egg roll with it. The wife likes that one." He smiled a bit then. I liked him; gruff but courteous enough.

So I took Cass, my duffel bag, and my guitar up to the room. Phoned my mother and informed her I wouldn't arrive until late morning the next day, or perhaps even early afternoon. She was disappointed. I could hear it in her voice. Felt it in the static on the line. Disappointed; too bad—I wasn't. I looked around the room after I hung up. It was dated but clean. No danger of picking up crabs or plantar warts. Overbearing orange and brown plaid curtains matched the bedspread. Smoke-stained wallpaper with peach-coloured flowers on it picked up the colour of the shag carpet. I opened a pack of Number 7s and sparked one up. An ashtray sat on the desk beside a lamp with a tacky gold lampshade. Obviously smoking was still allowed here; one of the few places left. Might as well take advantage of it. I just sat there and looked around as I inhaled the cigarette; there was no television in the room. That was fine; I'd brought a book anyway. I would just read when I got back from supper. *No One Here Gets Out Alive* was the name of the book. Read it once already many years ago. Found it again just recently. It's a good book. Great book, actually. Deemed it worthy of reading again.

"Okay, like, I'm really hungry, girl," I said to Cassie as I kissed the top of her head and rubbed the scruff of her neck. "I'm gonna go grab somethin' to eat, and then I'll be back." I threw on the leather jacket, I'd removed mere moments before. I was famished. "I'll bring you something back too."

I stepped out onto the cracked sidewalk that skirted the hotel. It was near the middle of March, but a chill hung heavily in the air. I shoved my hands deep in the pockets of my jeans as I strolled toward the lights of the only open business. Grocery store, gas station, even a bank—all closed and locked up for the night. It wasn't much of a walk. Wasn't much of a town, either. A thousand people at the very most. A classic Joni Mitchell song sprang to mind as I approached the greasy glass door of the restaurant, and I sang to myself about dreaming on dimes in the Chinese café.

Two old ladies, one with rollers in her hair, gave me the strangest look as they exited the restaurant. Who was the strange rocker-man walking the streets of the town they called home? I smiled at them. They glared. I snickered softly and sat down. There was no one in the place but me and the little Chinese girl in turtleneck and jeans who meandered to my table.

"I'll have combination B. The one with the egg roll," I told her, without even glancing at the menu wedged between the sugar jar, the soy sauce and the foggy salt and pepper shakers.

She smiled and nodded and sauntered away. Didn't say a word, just smiled and sauntered.

The tiny café was small, intimate, reasonably clean, but not immaculate—much like the hotel. Big, garish, red Chinese lanterns and multicoloured dragons hung overhead. Fat ugly Buddhas squatted on shelves with other

Asian bric-a-brac, and sprawling, smoke-stained fans adorned the walls. It was all geared to make the patrons of the establishment feel like they'd been magically transported to the exotic Far East instead of the middle of Canada's snow-swept grain-belt. I suppose it worked to a degree.

The Chinese girl plunked down a glass of ice water and some cutlery in front of me. I turned to see a tiny, stooped little man stir-frying vegetables in the open kitchen behind her. Steam from the grill fogged up his glasses. He, like the hotel proprietor, appeared weathered and old before his time. I knew how they felt. I was only a year away from turning forty, and some days I felt so much older that. I, like them, was a small business owner. Though mostly it's been very rewarding, it's also been a lot of work, long hours and stress. I own and manage a small used record shop. Dead Rock Stars, that's what I named the store. It's nothing fancy, but we buy, sell and trade used vinyl, cassette tapes, and compact discs. We also sell posters, buttons and t-shirts. It's a decent living. It'd never make a guy rich, but it's paid the mortgage on my condo and bought me a car and put food in mine and Cassie's bellies for years. And it's been easier since I hired Jim and Ray. I've been good to them and vice-versa. One is a student, works only part-time. The other works full-time. Has for years. He's a lifer, I think. Vinyl is his life. Not such a bad life. It's helped support him and his wife and their young family, too.

The little Chinese girl came back around again. She plunked a huge plate of food down in front of me and still didn't say a word. Hungry as I was, I ate quickly; gooey battered shrimp, sweet and sour ribs, chicken chow mein, fried rice, and the egg roll, of course. I ate about two-thirds then asked for a take-out container. Cassie could feast on the leftover chow mein and the steamed rice that I didn't even touch. She'd like that. I'd become very particular about what I fed the old girl. She was nine and starting to show her age. I fed her only lean meats, veggies and rice. I asked the waitress, who I had come to gather was the cook's daughter, for the bill.

For the first time since I'd walked into the café, she actually spoke. "Be right back," she said.

At the cash register I handed her a couple of folded bills. She handed me a fortune cookie in return. Told her to keep the change as the cool breeze from the street once again hit me in the face.

I still don't know what possessed me to do what I did next. It wasn't like me at all. I'm not a bar person. Not even at home in Saskatoon. Never go to bars, either gay or straight. Yet that night when I got back to the hotel, sleepy-eyed with Styrofoam container in hand, something about that dingy little small-town pub atmosphere beckoned me, and I found myself strolling into the lounge instead of heading directly up the stairs to Cassie. I knew she wouldn't mind. She'd waited this long for supper, she wouldn't mind being patient a little longer.

BROWN-EYED HANDSOME MAN

A YOUNG GUY was tending bar that night; his appearance suggested he was probably the owner's son. He looked to be in his twenties, unshaven, over-weight—not particularly attractive, but just friendly enough, like his father. A cap was pulled down low over his greasy blond hair.

"What'll it be?" he asked. Blunt like his dad too.

"Rum and Coke. Dark rum."

Tasteless clocks, lit beer signs and whisky logos added patches of light to the dark faux wood panelling that enveloped the dim room. Fewer people were around now than before I went for supper. I glanced at the Labbatt's Lite clock behind the bar. Ten thirty; late for people to be out on a week night. It was, after all, only Thursday. There would be work in the morning. And school. It didn't take me long to polish off my cocktail. I was already rising from the stool when I heard a voice.

"Buy you another?"

I turned. Another hat, this one a little different. A traditional cowboy hat. Black felt. Looked good on him. A dark, mildly-unkempt mustache flattered the deep-brown tan of his face. It was a real tan, too, the kind that comes from long hours of hard work in the prairie sun and wind. He had the type of leathery complexion a guy gets from exposure to extreme cold and heat. His denim shirt was open, revealing a forest of black hair; one of those beautifully enticing chests you just want to rest your head on for a while. He was probably about the same age as me.

"Mind if I join you?" he asked.

"I was just about to go up to my room. My dog's waiting for me," I said, a bit startled, looking down at the take-out container next to my empty glass on the bar.

"What kinda dog you got?" he asked with a smile. Oh, that smile.

"She's a lab."

"A lab? Bet she's a beauty," he said, pulling out the stool beside me and sitting down. "Clarence, how 'bout another beer? And one more of whatever my new friend 'ere is drinkin'" He turned back to me. "I got a couple dogs too. On my farm. No purebreds like yours, though. Big ol' Heinz 57s. Mangy things. But I like 'em. They're my family, know what I mean? Just me out there. Me and the animals. Them, the horses, a few cats. We all get along good. Good thing. Gets lonely out there by myself." He took a huge swig of beer. "So, where ya from?"

I was intoxicated and it wasn't because of the liquor. I told him where I was from. Told him a lot of stuff. Told him my life story, more or less; who I was, where I was going, why I was going there. I felt like I'd known him for years. Wished I had.

And after about a half-hour of conversation he surprised me. Really surprised me.

"I'd like to see her," he said.

"See who?"

"Yer dog. Never seen a chocolate lab. I'd like to meet 'er."

Oh, my. Was he putting the moves on me? *Me?* Was I, Jackson Hill, who rarely got laid back in the city, really being hit on by a swaggering wrangler in this dime-a-dozen little hotel bar in the middle of absolute nowheres-fucking-ville?

Suddenly, I wasn't sleepy anymore. Wasn't tired at all. Curious? Maybe. Flattered? Definitely. Mesmerized? Absolutely!

"Come on up," I said.

So he did. He just followed me up the steep, white-washed stairs to the little room and watched as Cassie devoured her long-awaited supper, giving her some pats after she was done. He sat on the edge of the bed; there was really nowhere else to sit.

"She's a sweetie," he said, smiling as he looked down at her. Oh, God, that smile. "You can tell," he continued, giving her a gentle rub. "It's in her stance, and her eyes; she's gentle and kind. Like you," he added, looking me directly in the eye. "Dogs are like that, ya know? They adopt the personalities of their masters. Shows what sensitive, devoted beings they are. How much they love their owners. Enough to be like 'em."

I found myself hanging on his words. Not only was he drop-dead gorgeous, he was fascinating. I groped for something to say. "I gotta take her outside for a minute," was all I could come up with.

"Go ahead," he said, "I'll wait here." He obviously had no thought of leaving anytime soon.

So I took Cassie outside. I put her on a leash—you never knew what'd happen in a little town like this; if she were to see a cat or even a jackrabbit or something come wandering out of the bush, she'd take off after it. She still had that much life in her. Then I'd have to go chasing after her and that wouldn't be good. I inhaled another cigarette while she sniffed the snow and found the perfect spot to piss on. I finished my smoke quickly, the chill in the air biting deeper with every minute and my thoughts on the warmth of the little room upstairs.

I wasn't disappointed.

He had removed his hat, along with the rest of his clothes, and lay in the soft light of the tacky gold lampshade, nestled in white sheets, his black hair cascading onto his shoulders a bit. I was entranced by his beautiful rug of dark chest hair and his endless smile. A young Waylon Jennings—that's who he reminded me of. I couldn't tear my gaze from him.

"Tell me somethin'," he said softly. "Yer dog here, what's 'er name?"

"Cass."

"That's nice."

"I named her after Mama Cass. You know, the singer from The Mamas and the Papas?"

He nodded, smiling. "Thought I'd spend the night here with you. That is, if you don't mind?"

"I don't mind," I replied. I noticed then how he'd piled his jeans and shirt on the floor on top of his scuffed cowboy boots, next to my guitar case. It would have made a nice still-life painting.

"Glad to hear it." He tilted his head to the window. "Saw you down there, sneakin' a puff. You wouldn't have had to do that. I wouldn't care if you lit up here. Used to have the same habit," he said, gently scratching Cassie's back until she curled up beside him on the creaky old bed. "Ya know, we don't have to do anythin' here tonight. In fact, wouldn't bother me one bit if we didn't. Just thought it'd be nice if we could spend the night together, if it's all right with you."

"It's all r-right," I stammered. This was definitely *not* how I'd expected to spend the evening, but I sure wasn't going to complain. Feeling like I was walking on clouds, I made my way to the cramped little bathroom and brushed my teeth with quivering hands.

I could hear him in the other room.

"It's probably all for the best anyways. I've had way too much to drink tonight to drive back to the farm."

"How far is it from here?" I inquired, exiting the washroom in nothing but my white jockeys, my hands awkwardly attempting to mask the raging boner his presence had given me.

"You know what's kind of funny?" he said, ignoring my question. "I like you so much. I'm just *comfortable* here with you and we've already told each other so much about ourselves—and yet I don't even know yer name."

"Jackson," I said. "But my friends call me Jack." It seemed the appropriate time for it had already passed, but I closed the few steps between us and extended my hand anyway.

"Pleased to meet you, Jack," he said. "I'm Frank." He reached out too.

The handshake felt good. One of those rare, solid handshakes when you can feel the energy in the room. One of those handshakes you know could be the start of a beautiful friendship. One of those handshakes that leads to a kiss. One of those kisses when you can smell the musk of his skin and the beer on his breath. One of those kisses that sets your heart on fire and puts your soul at ease. One of those kisses you wish could last forever.

Waylon Jennings. Another dead rock star in his own right.

A NEW SENSATION

JACKSON HILL, you are an *idiot!* A total idiot! Where was your brain last night? In your zipper, that's where!

I was so busy reprimanding myself for what had happened the night before that I nearly ran the stop sign as I left the little town. Nearly smashed into a bus full of kids on its way to school and was very grateful I hadn't. It was snowing; more blustery than the day before. Spring wasn't in the air today—it had been put on hold for the time being. That's how things go in these parts.

Frank Zabitzky was weighing on my mind. Woke up early that morning to find him gone. Gone from that creaky old bed in that cozy little room. Left a note telling me he had to get home to feed his horses. His phone number was scribbled on the same piece of paper, left on the pillow where his beautiful head had rested the night before. He'd left his smell too. His sultry, sensual smell lingered on the crisp white sheets and in Cassie's fur. On my body too. On my face, on my lips. Left his presence on my mind. His gentle face, his swagger, his charisma—all so memorable.

I manoeuvered the old green Rabbit down the snow-filled highway. Get him out of your head, Jack. Get him out fast. He's from another world. He's a farmer. He's a farmer *in the middle of nowhere!* You have a life in the city. You have a life of your own, miles and miles away from here. The back and forth swish of the windshield wipers was hypnotic. Oh, but he was so kind. So considerate. So friggin' hot. That's what it was. It was a physical thing. It was a one-night stand. Yeah, a one-night stand, even though there'd been no actual sex. Just talking, and laughing, and holding and kissing. Oh, those kisses—how they lingered in my mind. Franklin Zabitzky, I've only just met you, and I daresay I could easily fall in love. Oh, Jackson. Jackson, Jackson, Jackson—you're in trouble now. You're in trouble deep.

I had the sweetest hangover.

Cassie eyed me adoringly. I knew what she wanted: breakfast. There was plenty of dry dog food packed for her to munch on, but I knew if I brought it out from the hatch, she wouldn't really touch it. She was spoiled and we both knew it. After an hour or so on the road, I pulled into a gas station, one of those well-established roadside businesses where a traveller can meet all his needs in one brief stop: use the bathroom, check the oil, fill up the gas tank, and fill up the stomach as well. I was there for only a half-hour. My plate of sausage, scrambled eggs, rye toast and pan-fried hash browns were served by a friendly yet curt, gum-chewing waitress. Before I knew it, I was back on the road. I'd left most of the sausage and a bit of the eggs, and Cass enthusiastically ate the leftovers out of a take-out box in the backseat.

I glanced at my watch. Eleven. A couple more hours on the highway and I would be walking into the home I grew up in. My brothers and their wives would probably come over this afternoon. They might even be there waiting when I arrived. At last my thoughts turned away from Frank and toward what the rest of the day held in store. Austin and his wife Coral, and Noel and his wife Olive would be assembled in my mother's huge, country-style kitchen, sitting at the long oak table, sipping coffee and devouring home-made baking. Planning my father's funeral.

Oh, I guess I haven't mentioned that yet. My father is dead. He died two days before I left on this trip. He'd been shoveling a path through the snow from the garage to the house when he succumbed to a massive heart attack.

I hadn't cried yet. It just seemed like there were too many other things to do: making certain the guys at my shop had everything they needed for the next few days, having my one and only suit dry-cleaned, getting a haircut, giving my old guitar a proper tuning, packing. Getting on the road, too, and making sure the slippery highway didn't stop me from getting there. Getting picked up by a cowboy in some small-town bar. Yup, lots to do.

Dad was a good man. Hell, Dad was a *great* man. Maybe he'd seemed cold and distant while I was growing up, but he'd had things on his mind. A high-maintenance farm, a high-maintenance wife, three sons to raise. Three very rowdy, active, dramatically different sons. But Owen Hill had done his best. He'd had a very simple, sheltered upbringing himself, and was naive about a lot of the aspects of child-rearing. What does a father do when his sons are in conflict? What does he do when they're bullied at school or worse, are bullying someone else? Going through puberty, going on first dates, that kind of stuff—what to do then? What to do when you find out your youngest boy is a queer? What to do when you find out you're raising a homosexual? Right out here. Right out here in the middle of obscurity, in the middle of the bald, empty prairie.

Which brings me to the main reason I never want to make the drive out here. The real reason I have only ventured back on rare occasions; only one Christmas out of about every three and the odd Thanksgiving or school re-union. I had the perfect excuses: "Busy time of year at the shop, Mom, can't really get away." "The weather's real bad, Mother. I hate driving in blizzards, but I'll send you guys a parcel, all right?" It's all because of memories. That's the real reason my hometown holds no solace for me. Memories of not getting along with my siblings. Memories of not getting along with the other boys at school. The way people could never understand me. The way I didn't fit in. The way townsfolk could never see that I was still a boy growing into a man—just a different kind of man.

Anwar Changella. Now *he* was a man. Oh, he'd only been a boy, but at the time he'd *seemed* like a man. I'd been in the ninth grade. Freshman year—the year a boy's hormones really go wild.

I remembered it like it was yesterday. The first day of another dreary school year. About twenty or so classmates and I were assembled in the classroom, less than anxious for our homeroom teacher to walk in. There was all the usual stuff going on: girls talking about their summers as they enthusiastically organized their new pencil cases and put on lip gloss. Guys talking about the fast-approaching harvesting and hunting season and which girls they planned to pursue. Spit balls flew; kids had already made blow-guns out of their pens.

I had heard we had a new town doctor. I had heard he was East Indian. I had even heard he had a beautiful young wife and a few children, the oldest a boy about my age. But I was in no way prepared for the moment Anwar walked into my Grade 9 homeroom right before Mr. Novakowski came in and called the class to order. Anwar was tall and dark and mysterious. He wasn't like the other boys, I could tell that right away. I could tell by the way he wore his hair longer than any other guy at school. I could tell by the two striking beaded bracelets that hung intertwined from his wrist. I could tell by the way his crisp flannel shirt had been left unbuttoned and just hung loose around his jeans, and by the INXS T-shirt beneath it. The band's fresh, unconventional sound was just beginning to garner them fame.

I remember thinking Anwar was red hot, just like the band's lead singer, Michael Hutchence. Hot and cool at the same time, that was the best way to describe him. I was taken by the way he'd boldly strolled past all the other kids: farm boys who didn't know what to make of him; girls who wanted to get to know him. He just sauntered past them, a tiny stud earring in his ear and a guitar case on his back. He took the only vacant desk, the one in front of me. I wasn't the most popular kid by any means, so it wasn't as if anyone else had been anxious to sit there.

And I especially remember his smile, that illuminating white smile, when he turned around and I heard his low, sultry voice. "Is this desk taken?"

Michael Hutchence: another dead rock star.

WALKING ON THE MOON

I BEAT THE STORM. The snow had only really begun swirling in the last half-hour before I began the descent down the long tree-lined driveway of my parents' sprawling farm. My mother was already holding the squeaky front door of the old two-storey farmhouse open for me before I could even park the little compact car behind her minivan, pulling in alongside my brother's half-ton truck. The wind sent her grey bob of hair whipping around her face. She looked thin and tired in a black sweater and denim skirt that hung almost to her ankles.

"Mom, get inside—it's miserable out here," I admonished as I attempted to get Cass and my duffel bag out of the car. Before I knew it, my sisters-in-law, Coral and Olive, were in the doorway as well, grabbing my things out of my hands. I guess they figured I needed the help. Or perhaps they were merely glad to see me. Either way, I thought it amusing how the girls rushed to assist me. As if they were used to it all. Let the wife do it. Wife's a piece of shit but she better have supper on the table at five sharp; that always seems to be the attitude in these parts.

One thing about my parents' home, it was consistent. Nothing much ever seemed to change. The huge kitchen with the open dining room off to the side was still welcoming. Still full of ornaments and knickknacks; ceramic critters, dried flower arrangements, and hanging plants in the windows. Bright yellow walls with yellow gingham curtains to match. Ironic how a kitchen can seem so bright and sunny when you can see a blizzard obliterating the view right outside the large window over the sink.

"We were just about to have coffee," Mom said, embracing me.

I inhaled it then, the warm, comforting smell of a cup of joe. That, combined with the scent of fresh baking and the pine cleaner my mother's kitchen always smelled of, brought back the years of my youth.

"Have you had lunch? We just finished, but there's a lot of food here. The neighbours keep sending stuff over. I really don't know what to do with it all."

"Just coffee, thanks, Mom," I answered, "I had a mountainous breakfast on the road." I hugged Olive and then Coral too, while Cassie wandered into the living room to stretch out. "Where is everyone?" By that I meant my brothers. I knew my nieces and nephew would be at the nearby community high school. Each couple had two teenagers.

"The guys are in town, running some errands," Coral replied.

"That right?" I answered.

Coral looked a lot like her sister Olive. Both dressed the same; casual, yet feminine. Warm, fuzzy turtlenecks and jeans covered their trim bodies. They had the same hairstyle too; just past shoulder-length and worn in a ponytail. The only major physical difference between them was the colour of their hair. Coral kept hers light brown, while Olive always lightened hers to a golden blond. Yep, my sisters-in-law are sisters. Some people might find that strange, but in these parts it's very common; siblings marrying siblings, or at least dating them.

The four of us settled into visiting. It was real visiting, where the love and comfort we found in each other's company could actually be felt in the room as we sipped hot coffee, had some laughs and shed a few tears. I'd always liked my brothers' wives, and enjoyed their companionship. Perhaps that's why I felt so violated when my brothers pulled in. Perhaps I just wasn't yet ready to allow them into our inner circle. I watched them barrel down the gravel driveway in another half-ton.

"Well, look who's here!" called Noel as he banged the door open, dripping muddy water from his work boots all over the polished white linoleum.

Unlike Austin, he hadn't bothered to stop at the front porch to remove his coat. Maybe that was because he was too excited to see me. But somehow I doubted it. More like he was anxious to get the greeting over with. Austin came in behind him and shook my hand across the kitchen table. They helped themselves to coffee and pulled up chairs.

The visiting resumed, my father's absence felt by all. We spoke of him a lot, though. The funeral too; where it would take place the next day, what time, who would be there. We talked of farming, my brothers' children, their homes, this house, what would happen now, what Mom's plans were.

Finally, Coral turned and asked me a question. "So what about you, Jacky? What's going on in your life? Anyone special? How's business at the shop, by the way?"

"It's good," I said, finishing the last drop in my mug. "Very good, actually. Keeps me busy. Actually, so busy I don't have time for much else. By the time I get home at the end of the day, and run Cass and make supper, I'm really too exhausted for much else." I was proud of my response. It answered the question quite properly and managed not to open up too much.

The rest of them resumed chattering and planning, but Coral kept her attention on me. "C'mon, Jack. Let's take Cassie for a walk."

I'd always thought of my parents' place as scenic and beautiful, even though I've always known, in my heart of hearts, that the rural life was not for me. Farm life, with its balance of drudgery and reward, is a good one for lots of people, but it simply wasn't for me. The wind was dying down and the snow now fell lightly. I thought it breathtakingly beautiful, actually, how it covered the roof of the big red barn at the back of the yard and the vehicles and the swather and all the other machinery. How it just covered it all.

"You didn't answer my question," Coral broke the silence.

"I didn't?"

"Not entirely," she said, smiling down at Cassie sniffing the snow. Cass was unaccustomed to being out in the middle of the prairie. Hell, so was I. We were like two disoriented explorers in unknown alien territory. We headed down the driveway and onto the gravel road. A farm truck drove by and the driver waved. Coral waved back. Obviously, she knew him.

"It's hard to believe Dad's gone. I'll miss him. He was a good man," I said. "Not perfect or anything, but he was a good man."

"Yes, he was," she said. "Do you have a smoke?"

"Yeah."

"I could really use one."

"Me too," I said, handing her a cigarette and lighting it for her before lighting my own. "Thought you quit like everyone else these days."

"I did," she replied. "It's just that I'm a little stressed. Helping plan the funeral. We're all kind of clueless about this stuff. I'm really glad you're here now. The city guy come to rescue us country folks."

"I don't know how much help I'll be. I…Coral, are you all right?"

Her eyes were wet. Her nose was running.

"I don't know. I think so." Her voice cracked.

"What is it?" The snow was falling harder again. I threw my hood over my head then reached over to cover her head with her own.

"Oh, it's lots of things. Owen dying. I really loved him. He's been like a father to me, too. My own dad died so long ago now." She wiped her cheeks with a tissue she found in the pocket of her parka. "I…I want to leave your brother. I want to separate."

"Really?" I asked, somewhat taken aback.

"Really," she answered. "I've felt this way for a long time. I don't want this anymore. I don't want any of it."

"I don't know what you mean."

"The twins are graduating this spring, you know."

"I know."

"They've already sent applications away to different universities. Their marks are really good. Honour roll and all that. They're bound to get in. Even have their choice. They'll be gone in just a few short months," Coral gently turned me around at the crossroads and we began walking back to the farm.

"You'll miss them," I said.

"More than you can imagine," she replied, passion in her voice. "You know, when I was the girls' age, I had none of the desires they do; they want to see the world, they want to get educated. Me, I just wanted to stay here and marry a nice farmer and raise some kids."

"And that's what you did."

"Yeah," she looked away. "That's what I did."

"And now?"

Her tears began to fall once again. "Now? Oh, I don't know. I just keep thinking, what's it all about? Austin wants to take over your dad's land now. Him and Noel. They want to farm it all. They're even eyeing more equipment at the dealership. They want to invest in a new combine."

"And that's bad?"

"It's not *bad*, it's just, I feel so…stagnant. Like life has passed me by and I've done nothing with it. Austin is a good man. A decent, hardworking man, a good provider…" she trailed off, staring into a frozen field. Suddenly she giggled. "But he's boring as hell, Jack!"

We both laughed.

"Noel's the fiery one. And Olive seems to like that about him. They're both hot-heads. They have that love-hate thing going."

"True."

"And you, you're the artistic one. The contemplative, creative one. That's what makes you so interesting."

"I suppose," I nodded.

"And Austin's just…well, really dull. He's boring me to death." She laughed and cried at the same time then.

I put my arm around her and gave her a quick squeeze.

We strolled in warm, comfortable silence in the frosty afternoon, in the kind of peace that exists when two very old friends are reunited for the first time in a long time. When they are just so content to be with each other there's no need for words.

Finally though, she broke the stillness. "Remember when we were all back in high school?"

"How could I forget?"

"We always had so much fun. Remember all those jam sessions after school in my parents' garage? Those were the days, Jack. They really were. You and Anwar on guitar. That Krochuk kid on drums. I forget his name."

"Billy."

"Yeah, that was it."

"And your singing was always enchanting," I added.

"Oh, I don't know if 'enchanting' is the word," she laughed.

"No really, it was very good. We all were."

"We were gonna be *famous.*"

"You were gonna be the next Karen Carpenter."

She giggled again. "Oh boy, was I ever. She was my idol. Still is."

"You really did sound a bit like her. Looked a little like her, too." I gave her a thoughtful perusal. "You still do, actually."

More silent strolling and then, "You know, Jack, it was you I really liked at first. Not Austin. Not at first."

"Really?" I exclaimed, choking on the last of my cigarette, completely surprised.

"Yeah, really," she said, mildly embarrassed. "Even though you were a couple grades below me, I—I always found you alluring. Maybe because I knew. I…knew it could never be."

"What do you mean?"

"You and Anwar. I knew. Long before anyone else. I had it all figured out, you know."

I looked up to see that we had arrived back at the house. Good thing. The chill was seeping in and I wasn't certain if I was ready to carry on this particular conversation.

Karen Carpenter: another dead rock star.

I WANNA BE SEDATED

MY BROTHERS EVENTUALLY took their wives home. They loaded up their big pick-up trucks with extra casseroles and baking and headed out. There would be kids to feed and chores to do. Mom and I kept busy going through her fridge and figuring out which of the remaining dishes we would have for supper, finally deciding on the perogies Mrs. Sankas had sent over, and the holobchi from the Levinskis just up the road. The saskatoon berry pie Olive had brought would make a nice dessert. We ate comfortably at the bulky dining room table, Cassie at my feet, anticipating some food herself.

"I figured you'd want to sleep in your old room," Mom said as she played with the pathetically little bit of food on her plate. "So I laundered the sheets in there. I gave the whole room a good cleaning too. It's good. Gave me something to do."

"Well, if I know you, it didn't need cleaning," I said, grinning. I think I was trying to keep her spirits up.

She smiled too. "Oh, I bet your place is spotless too. I bet you're a bit of a neat freak yourself. You were always tidy as a boy."

"I suppose. I never seem to mess anything up. Never have time," I said, getting up to see if there was anything in the fridge to drink.

"The store keeps you that busy?"

"Boy, does it ever," I nodded, pouring myself a glass of water from a pitcher in the refrigerator.

My mother put her fork down, even though she'd hardly touched a thing on her plate. "It's funny," she said, her voice low. "When you were all kids, I really thought you would become a professional musician. I always figured that would be your career."

I devoured the last of the meal quickly. That old feeling was beginning to wash over me, my self-esteem dwindling until I felt like a piece of shit.

She took her plate to the sink and returned to the table with the pie. She cut into it slowly.

I stared out the dining room window. It always amazed me how quickly darkness fell out here in the country, and how black it became. Much darker than in the city. Couldn't see much of anything even though the overbearing yard light was on.

She continued. "I always thought you'd be the one. Of all my boys, *you'd* be the one who'd really make it in the outside world."

"I like to think I have," I said, swallowing a forkful of pie. I was really quite anxious now to finish the meal, clean up the kitchen, get Cass fed and outside to do her business, then curl up in bed with her. It had been such a long day. A very long day, actually, and not much sleep the night before. Not much sleep with Frank Zabitzky in my bed, that's for sure.

"Well, of course."

I could tell she didn't really agree with me. Could tell by the tone of her voice. By the way she looked away, toward the bleakness out the window, and the way she avoided my eyes as she spoke.

Perhaps that's why, a couple hours later when I still hadn't fallen fast asleep as I was so certain I would, I lifted the patchwork quilt I lay under and ventured back into the darkness of the kitchen. I grabbed the cordless phone and crept back to my old room, holding my breath as I stole past Mom's bedroom on the main floor and up the squeaky steps. Grabbing my jeans from the armchair by the dresser, I pulled the piece of paper from the front pocket and dialed the number scrawled on it.

"Hello?" I heard after one quick ring.

"Hi, Frank."

"Jack!"

"Were you sleeping?"

"Not quite. Reading a book. Kind of drifting off. Glad you called."

"You read?"

"All the time. What are you doin'?"

I found his voice so soothing I didn't even want to answer his questions; I'd rather just listen to him for a while.

"Lying in my old bed, trying to sleep," I replied anyway, looking around the room, seeing how little it had changed in the years I'd been gone. It was pretty much the same, except for the rock band posters I'd once had strewn all over the walls.

"Memories?"

"Memories."

"Good or bad?"

"Both."

"Wanna talk about them?"

"I don't know."

"I've been thinkin' a lot about you."

"Oh? And what'd you come up with?"

"I really like you, Jack."

"I…like you too."

"I'm glad."

"Could never work, you know, you and me," I finally said, trying to keep it real.

"Why not?"

"We're worlds apart."

"I wouldn't say worlds."

"I own a business and a house in the city. You own a farm almost two hundred miles away."

"Ever been in love, Jackson?"

The question surprised me. "Yes. Once."

"Hopelessly?"

"Yes."

"Was it enough? I mean, was it everything you thought it'd be?"

"Yes."

"Then why ain't you together?"

"He…died."

"I'm sorry," he said, and it sounded like he meant it.

I was finally starting to feel tired, like I could maybe sleep. "It's all right. It was a very long time ago. You?"

"Once."

"What happened?"

"Oh, well, the chemistry was there. It's just…he had some problems. Drugs, alcohol—that kinda thing. He left me to go work it all out, even though I wanted him to stay. He told me he couldn't. Said he was damaged goods. "

"So…he just left one day?"

"Yeah, that's what he did. I told him damaged goods are just like anything else in the world. Everyone, even him, deserves to be loved. Funny. We met through an ad in the paper. Even in this age of internet dating and chat rooms. Met through the classifieds."

"So you mean he lived out there with you?"

"Yup. Moved out of the city away from his parents' to live here and farm with me."

"He thought that's what he wanted?"

"Yup. And I think it *was* what he wanted. At least then. He was young. We both were."

I needed to know. "How did the town treat you guys?" I asked. I was grateful for his my-life-is-an-open-book attitude. So refreshing.

"Pretty good, all in all. Oh, they all gossiped about us for a while. And then they got used to it. That's how people are. They adjust. I…" he trailed off, then finished in a rush of words, "I could come down there, ya know."

"What?"

"I could come down there. I mean, if you think it'd help. If you need a friend."

"Oh," I laughed nervously, "I don't know."

"Just sounded like you could use someone. I miss you, Jack."

"You do?"

I could hear his smile. "I do. I've been thinkin' 'bout you all day."

"Really?"

"Yeah."

"And what do you think?"

"I think you're amazing. I think you're warm and unique and, well, very easy on the eyes."

"Funny. I could say the same things about you."

"Ya know, last night before we met, I saw you. I was driving past Ming's Café. I had just left my mother's in town. I check on her almost every day. Make sure she's all right. Thought I'd make a quick trip down Main Street and see what was happening. And there you were, sittin' in the café. All by yer lonesome. I said to myself, 'Franklin, that looks like an interesting man. Good lookin' one too. One worth stoppin' and gettin' to know. Even if it turns out his bread ain't buttered on the same side as yours, still looks like he'd be interesting to talk to.'"

"You followed me?" I asked, my voice rising slightly in shock.

"Sorta. I figured if you were stayin' in town, you'd need a drink before goin' on up to yer room. Figured if I went to the hotel bar, you might show up there eventually."

"And I did."

"Yeah, ya did. I'm glad."

"Me too."

"Good."

"Listen, I'd better go. I'm really wiped out," I paused for a moment. "Thank you, Frank, for…well, everything."

"All right. Call me again anytime, Jack."

"I will."

"You could stop here you know," he said suddenly. "On yer way back to the city. You could stop here and I could show you my farm."

I chuckled. "Your animals too?"

"Yup. I got it all. Cattle, horses, dogs. You like horseback ridin'?"

"I don't know."

"What do you mean you don't know? Didn't you guys have horses on yer farm when you were growin' up?"

"No. We were strictly grain farmers."

"Really? And my dad was a cattle farmer. He died a few years back. Now I'm the sole owner of the place. My mom's got herself a little house in town. It all worked out pretty good. Ya know, you could try it when you stop here."

"Try what?"

"Horseback ridin'. I think you'd love it. There's a beautiful meadow here. It's nicer in the summer, but we could get on Cherry and Chestnut and go for a ride through there. I'd put you on Chestnut. He's older. More patient. I think you'd get along good."

"Sounds wonderful. But I really better go now." I was fading fast.

"All right, then. Sleep well, Jackson."

"You too."

"G'night, Jack."

"Good night."

I fell asleep finally. A peaceful, restful slumber of hypnotic dreams of horseback riding with Frank, perched high atop Cherry and Chestnut, racing through a sunlit meadow.

UNDER PRESSURE

I AWOKE ON SATURDAY in a state of confusion. I'd fallen into such a deep sleep that I was completely disoriented when I first opened my eyes. This was the room I'd slept in night after night until my eighteenth summer. I felt like a ghost in it now. For years, I had avoided my parents' home like the plague. Not because I didn't love them or want to spend time with them. It was just because I liked my own space. I liked the home I'd made for myself in the city. The life I'd made for myself too. What real reason was there to drive hours and hours to this little hick town and sit around the house and do nothing?

My father was a very introverted man. He was always happy to see me, but what he really enjoyed was being out on his tractor or puttering in his wood shop, constructing birdhouses and lawn ornaments. He liked the company of his own friends and often made the short drive into town to sit on coffee row with the rest of the town's patriarchs in Fern's Café, joining them in the ongoing discussion of the price of grain and the latest hockey game.

What did he really have to talk about with his youngest son? I mean, what was he really supposed to say to me? "How's the shop been, Jacky?" "Do you have any original copies of the Beatles' *Abbey Road* album by any chance?

Or Bowie's *Ziggy Stardust and The Spiders from Mars*?" Or get this: "How's your love life, Jacky?"

No, those conversations would never happen.

I could hear noise from the kitchen as I slowly crawled out of bed: my mother making breakfast, Noel's loud, obnoxious voice and Austin's lower, more subdued one. From what I could hear, Mom was pouring them coffee and juice and buttering their toast. For fuck's sakes, didn't these guys ever give the woman a break? Why did they always have to be here? And why were the two of them always together? I knew their farms were only a couple miles away from each other, but why did they have to be together all the time? It was like some inbred hillbilly family you'd see on a trashy TV talk show.

Oh, just settle yourself down, Jackson. The funeral's today, you'll stay a day or two more and help get a few things in order, then you're out of here.

I grabbed a pair of sweats and a long-sleeved T-shirt out of my duffel bag, and Cass and I headed downstairs.

"I figured you were gonna sleep the whole day away!"

Oh, go screw yourself Noel, I thought, grinning so wide it hurt. "The service isn't until ten thirty," I muttered, a cool gust of air hitting me in the face as I threw Cass's leash on her, shoved my feet into my boots and opened the front door. "I'm just gonna take her out to pee, and I'll be right back."

"Whaddya gotta go with her for? She need you to piss?" he asked.

"Yeah," I said. I couldn't wait to get outside and light a smoke. Needed some coffee too. But with the mood Noel was in and the effect it was having on me, a cigarette outside in the fresh breeze was probably best. I knew that mood of his. Hell, I'd grown up with the man. He was thinking, *This is all mine now. Dad left it to me and Austin, and we're the kings of the town. Kings of the grain fields.* Miles and miles of dirty, dusty fields. Well, you can have it, Noel. You can have it all.

Back inside, I poured myself a steaming cup of coffee.

"You want some breakfast? Some toast? A muffin?" my mother asked as she jumped up from the table in her terry-cloth robe.

It's always amazed me out here—the women in these parts, I mean. Different from the city. How most of them are just *accustomed* to attending to the needs of the men in their lives, catering to their wants and desires.

"No, I'm fine," I said. "I'm not much for breakfast."

"Probably used to fancy-shmancy meals," Noel said. "Eggs Florentine 'n all that," he continued, stretching back in his chair.

"Where are Coral and Olive?" I asked, ignoring him and settling in at the table myself.

Noel was about to answer, but Austin cut him short. Perhaps he'd sensed my patience with Noel's arrogance was wearing thin. "The girls are at home, getting the kids and themselves ready for the funeral. But there's something the four of us need to discuss." Austin looked tired and stressed—dull, like Coral had said. His skin was pale and his blondish hair looked nearly white in the cold morning light. Well, I guess *his* father had just died too. You had to cut the guy some slack. Of all of us boys, Austin was probably the closest to my dad. He really loved him. Noel? Well, he was really too in love with himself to love anyone else.

I took a good swig of coffee, needing the caffeine in my system in order to focus on this conversation with my family.

"What's that?" I asked after I swallowed.

Mom shifted in her chair, uncomfortable and uneasy. "I guess the boys are going to take over the land," she said. "We've been discussing it for some time already. Your father and I and them."

"I figured that's what would happen," I said, nonchalant. "I mean, it only makes sense, doesn't it?"

My mother began clearing the table of soiled plates and half-empty jars of homemade jam. "And I'm going to move. I'm going to move to town, into those new duplexes Arnold Heinz built. He's having trouble renting them out anyway. That should all work out quite nicely."

"I don't see why you have to rush, Mom. You could stay for a while, you know."

She rubbed her shoulders as if she suddenly felt a chill. "I could but I don't want to, Jacky. Your father and I had a life here. A good life…" Her eyes took on a faraway look, then she looked down at her hands. "But it's over. It's time to move on now."

"Yeah, so we're gonna tear the place down," Noel jumped in. "No point in it sittin' here empty, just fallin' apart."

"Oh," I said. "End of an era, I guess." What else was there to say?

"Dad left it to you too, you know," Austin put in, his eyes boring into mine, trying to read me.

"Left what?" I asked.

"The farm. The land."

"Yup," muttered Noel. "Left it equally to the three of us."

"Really?" I'd had no idea.

"Yup. Wanted it all to be fair," he added, leaning forward on the table. "So the way I see it, you got a big decision to make."

"What's that?"

"Well a citified guy like you," and here he smirked, though I knew he wasn't just teasing, "ain't gonna move back down here and start farming." No one else spoke so he went on. "Way I see it, you can just go back up north to the city. Be a silent partner, you might say."

Mom was wiping the table now, clearing away toast crumbs and sugar granules. She seemed nervous. Austin just sat there and let Noel do all the talking.

"The other thing you could do is sell. Sell your third to us. That'd make the most sense."

"You'd really be rid of me then, wouldn't you?" I replied, stung.

"Jacky, that's not what we want," Mom said, sitting down to rejoin us. "It's just that this just seems like the logical way to go about things. The boys have to think about their livelihood."

"God forbid I should ever be part of the team," I said, speaking my thoughts out loud now. "God forbid there should *ever* be any unity among us."

Austin and my mother simply sat there, staring across the table at me. This was obviously between Noel and me.

"Oh, don't get your panties in a twist," he sighed in sudden exasperation. "We're just trying to come up with the most sensible solution to all this."

I looked at the clock on the kitchen wall. "I better get upstairs. I have to shave, shower…" I moved away.

"Don't go away angry, now," Noel belted out after me. "I'm sure that once you think about all this, you're gonna see selling is probably the best thing."

"I'm sure it is, Noel," I muttered. "I'm sure it is."

SUPERSTAR

THERE'S SOMETHING PREDICTABLE about family funerals; the way you know in your mind how it's all going to play out, exactly how everything will unfold.

I sat in the back room of the small church on the edge of town, one of three churches in the community. The small town had few denominations, sparse congregations assembling each Sunday morning to worship. I sat in the little family room and peered at those already in the pews through the lace curtains of the window dividing us and them. Relatives and townsfolk had gathered, waiting anxiously for us to appear. It was like we were the celebrities of the day. I found it amusing. It's like a rock concert, how the crowd waits in anticipation for the performance. And when we walked down the aisle to take our places at the front, that's when the show would really begin.

I knew my mother would be in her well-used black funeral dress, the one she's been wearing in recent years to say goodbye to the many people dearly departed: her mother, her mother-in-law, some aunts and uncles. After all, she's at that age now, that golden age when your friends and relatives really begin to die off. I knew Austin would sit quietly in the corner of the room, patiently waiting for this all to be over so he could go back to the quiet farm existence he preferred to lead. I knew Noel would strut around in some hideously mismatched dress clothes, quite content to be the centre of attention for the day. I knew their wives and my nieces and nephew would sit solemnly, tissues in hand and wearing their Sunday best, wiping tears from their cheeks. They were saying goodbye to someone who had been a big part of their lives. They had every right to be taking it hard.

Yes, I predicted all this. More people in the church than it could properly accommodate. The smell of incense just a little too strong. My father decked out in a suit he would have detested wearing, lying in an overpriced coffin at the front of the building. An organist was positioned a few feet away from him, playing Ian and Sylvia Tysons' "Four Strong Winds." I expected it all.

What I didn't expect was to have Frank Zabitzky come strolling into this little back room, clad in a black suit, bolo tie and cowboy boots, and go straight up to my mother and extend his hand.

"Hello, ma'am. You must be Jackson's mother. I'm Frank, a friend of his. I thought I'd come down here and join you, if it's all right with you."

The looks on my family's faces were fascinating; my mother, bewildered as to who this tall, dark cowboy was and wondering why he wanted to join the farewell to her husband. Austin wanting nothing more than to escape and go home to putter in his garage. And Noel, wearing his customary sneer, trying to intimidate the stranger invading our group. Coral and Olive and my nieces and nephew merely seemed fascinated with who this hot-looking stud might possibly be. Could Uncle Jacky have a *boyfriend*?

I introduced Frank to everyone in the cramped room, then feeling the urgent need for a smoke, I hauled him outside.

We stood outside the church and stared out toward the graveyard next door. A mound of dirt lay beside a hole dug in the half-frozen earth. In a very short while, my father's body would descend into it. Then it would be quickly covered with soil and snow. There was only a light fall today. Nothing like the days before. It was all so silent. No traffic, no people. I guess most of the community was inside the crowded church.

Frank spoke. "Well, at least the roads were good coming down. No sliding or anything. I just put new tires on…"

"What are you doing here?" I turned to him.

He was quiet for a few moments, then said, "I don't know. I just kept thinkin' about you. How you told me the other night in the bar that you never felt comfortable in this town. I just wanted to be here for you."

We stared at the graveyard and the icy road, and the town that lay beyond it; well-maintained homes with smoke billowing out of the chimneys, and freshly graded streets.

"You know, Jack, if you really don't want me here…I mean, if you'd prefer I get in my truck and drive home, I will. Just say the word and I'll leave you alone."

I looked at him. I smiled to myself. I bet he hated wearing that black suit. Bet he even hated not having a hat on. It was obvious from the tan line circling his slightly balding scalp that he was unaccustomed to being without something on his head. But he'd done it all for me; the suit, the long drive, meeting my family.

"I don't want you to go," I said softly.

Frank grinned. "You know what I don't understand?" he asked, starting to shiver just a bit.

"What's that?"

"You and yer brothers' names. They're…kind of unusual. 'Specially for a farmin' family out here in southern Saskatchewan."

I reefed on the stub my cigarette had become. "Well, I did warn you my parents were a little different," I replied, unable to stifle a smile. "Austin was named after the city in Texas. Mom and Dad went on a road trip through the States for their honeymoon and Dad told me that's where Austin was conceived."

Frank nodded. I could tell he found that entertaining.

"Noel was born on Christmas Eve. Maybe that's why I hate the season so much. Anyway, I guess that's why he's got girly-name syndrome."

Frank looked at me, baffled. "Whaddya mean?"

I took a final drag. "Girly-name syndrome. It's this complex guys who have feminine-sounding names get. I mean, look at John Wayne. The guy's name was Marion, for frig' sakes. The man spent his entire life trying to be this macho, bad-ass cowboy to compensate."

Frank busted right up. I was stunned by how much I liked this man. This man, who I was finding to be sincere and kind, educated in some ways but naive in others, worldly yet redneck, rugged but gentle. I tossed the butt of my smoke into the snow. "My name came from the song. You know, the Johnny Cash and June Carter tune. Dad told me they were beltin' it out on the radio when he was drivin' my mom to the hospital when she was in labour."

Frank nodded and grinned as he opened up the door to the church and motioned me to go in ahead of him. So we stepped out of the cold to re-join my family in the claustrophobic room. A few moments later, we walked down the main aisle of the sanctuary, filing into the front pews together, listening to the minister and the choir. My mother sat on one side of me, Frank on the other, his knee pressing ever so gently against mine.

I found it comforting, his presence beside me in this narrow church, despite so many others staring across the room at us, trying to figure us out. Who was the outsider with the black sheep of the Hill family? I wouldn't have had it any other way, though, finding solace in his suit jacket brushing softly against mine every now and again, and his warmth next to me—just far enough away to be politically correct but close enough for me to be aware of his woodsy cologne and the scent of his skin. I would have loved to just lean over and rest my tired head on his muscular shoulder.

And later, at the interment, as my dad's body was swallowed by the earth, Frank discreetly lay a warm hand on my back, and for the first time since I'd heard that my father had died, I cried.

STRUTTER

AFTERWARDS, IT SEEMED like half the community crowded into my mother's house. Many of the people from town made the short drive out to the farm, like they weren't quite prepared for it all to end. You would think that after the heartfelt service and the long stand in the freezing-cold cemetery, everyone would just want to head home. But here they all were, scattered throughout the large kitchen, filling the chairs in the dining room, overflowing the living room. The noise was almost deafening. I guess people had had enough of just sitting back and listening and contemplating; enough sadness, enough tears. Now there was lively conversation. Something Dad had always said kept springing to mind—laugh so you don't cry. But it *was* time to move on a bit. The formalities of death were over. Let us just remember the man, cherish the memories and move forward.

Coral and Olive were busy pulling food from the cramped fridge and setting up a buffet along the long kitchen counter. Homemade buns, sliced ham, Canadian cheddar cheese, pickles, macaroni salad, coleslaw; all the traditional mourning food. My mother was pouring water into a huge coffee percolator, already fretting about what the crowd would have for dessert. My nieces and several town women flitted in and out of the kitchen, attempting to assist but really only getting in the way. Too many cooks spoil the soup, my mother always said.

Frank had made himself useful in his own way as well, sitting in the living room, talking to various cousins and acquaintances. They spoke of farming, the price of grain, the price of cattle, and the price of fuel, and all the while he gave Cass some gentle rubs, keeping her company while I was busy elsewhere. The masses were warming up to him. How could they not? He had such charisma. He was one of them.

I was standing at the edge of the open kitchen, watching Frank smile in response to something his companion said, when Mom asked me to run down to the cellar to fetch some paper plates.

She'd certainly have her hands full when she moved, I thought, glancing around the partially finished basement. I stood in the cold room for the first time in years, taking it all in; more food than any elderly couple could possibly consume. Jars of pickled cucumbers and beets sat alongside preserved raspberries on one shelf. On the other were jams and marmalades above a heaping potato bin. Why did she always feel compelled to preserve this much food? But I guess we're all creatures of habit. She was so conditioned to hauling up the hefty black canner every autumn and preserving everything she possibly could from her massive garden.

I must have been down there for quite some time, trying to locate the disposable plates. I guess I was lost in thought, because before I knew it, Olive was down there too.

"Not having any luck?" she asked.

"No, I guess not," I agreed.

She reached up and lifted the bag of paper plates down from a shelf over my head. "I know this house pretty good. I know all your mom's hiding spots."

I pulled the string hanging from the bare light bulb and darkness filled the room as we walked out.

"So, Jacky, who *exactly* is that fabulous man?" Olive wanted to know, curiosity mingled with sincere concern in her eyes, as she halted at the bottom of the steep steps that led back to the kitchen.

"Oh, he's a new friend," I said, smiling a little sheepishly.

"A boyfriend or just a friend?"

"You know, I'm not sure yet."

"Well, he's charming as hell," she said, grinning.

"Isn't he just, though?" I grinned now too. That's one thing I always appreciated about Olive; she was direct and got right to the point. She looked terrific too, despite the fact she'd just been to a funeral. Her chocolate-brown jacket and skirt suited her, and her highlighted hair was meticulously done. Olive had never been quite as pretty as Coral but she'd always had a certain appeal. It was in her fiery personality, her confidence, and her spunk.

We heard the squeak of the upstairs door then. We looked up to see Noel thump down the stairs.

"You got a lot of nerve, little brother!"

"What do you mean?" I asked, bewildered.

"Bringin' some boyfriend down here and flauntin' him in front of the family and the whole goddamn town!"

"Noel, don't start anything." Olive kept her voice calm.

"You stay outta this," he ordered, pointing a finger at her. "This is between me and him." He turned his attention back to me. The cold hard cement at the bottom of the stairs seeped into my thin dress socks and I held back a shudder. "That's what I don't understand about you girly boys. How you gotta flaunt your sissy-ass relationships around in everyone's face."

"I think if anyone in this family likes to flaunt things, it's you," I responded. I was in no mood to capitulate.

"What the hell is *that* supposed to mean?" he demanded.

Olive stepped forward and stood directly between us. "Guys! Stop this! We just came home from your dad's funeral. We're all tired; it's been a rough time. I bet you don't even realize what you're saying—your emotions are just running high."

"Oh, I think Noel knows *exactly* what he's saying," I said, gently guiding her out of the way. "I think he's been wanting to say it for a very long time. Haven't you, Noel?"

"Jackson," he sneered, "you wanna live your life as a queer, you go right ahead." He waved a finger at me. "All I ask is that you not come down here and shove it in our faces!"

I took a deep breath. "Frank is a hundred times the man you are," I said, not backing down from him one little bit, raising my voice to compete with his. The hum of conversation upstairs lessened. Then I started laughing at the ridiculousness of it all. "You know, Noel," I said, "we don't have to do this anymore."

"Do *what?*" he demanded.

"Go around pretending we like each other. Putting on the act. We don't have to do it anymore. Dad's gone. That's really who we did it for anyway, isn't it? Keep the peace and all that. Mom, well, I don't think she really cares. You and Austin, you're her golden boys. As long as she's got the two of you a couple miles away to fawn over, she doesn't care about much else."

He stared at me, speechless. I'd managed to shut him up. Even Olive didn't seem to have anything much to say and she leaned back against the deep freezer. So I continued. "So the way I see it, after this weekend, we don't have to have anything to do with each other. You can buy me out like you said earlier, and I'll go back north and resume my life, and we don't ever have to deal with each other again."

Noel glowered at me, but couldn't find a thing to argue with. It was kind of funny, actually, though I didn't feel much like laughing.

"Come on," Olive said, pulling me toward the stairs. "Let's go up. Everyone's going to be wondering what's going on down here."

I went with her. Noel stayed put.

"Just gotta have the last word, eh, daisy-boy?" he muttered.

"You go ahead and have it. See if I care," I said, turning back.

"You know what I never understood about you, Jack?" he asked, waves of hostility radiating off him.

"What's that?"

"You and whatshisname. When he died. You could've saved him."

"Anwar," Olive said, finally losing patience. "His name was Anwar, Noel!"

"Whatever his name was." He waved her words away. "The way I hear it, you were only a few feet away from him. You never made the effort. Like it was okay for him to die or somethin'. Like you wanted it. Or even needed it. I think that's how your gearboxes work. You *like* drama and misery and all that."

Olive eyed me nervously.

For the first time in many years, I could feel a black rage rise up through the ground and into my body. I curled my long, musician's fingers into a fist, wound up, and sent my brother flying into the cement wall behind him in one good solid punch.

And at just that moment Mom opened the cellar door to see what was going on.

I readjusted my crooked glasses and marched up the stairs, leaving Olive to examine her husband's bloody nose. And when I reached the top of the steps, I couldn't help but turn around and get in the last word after all.

"You know what, Noel? All that stuff you said about me? Maybe it's true. Maybe I am a screaming fag, and maybe I am flaunting Frank around like a hyena with a fresh piece of meat, and maybe— just maybe—I *could've* saved Anwar…" I looked at my mother's face then, at the despair and the disappointment. And said it anyway. "But you know what, Noel? At least I didn't get the girly name!"

ROXANNE

THE CROWD DISPERSED soon after. Perhaps it was because the masses had been fed and they were anxious to get home to rest and relax. Perhaps it was because they'd heard raised voices and sensed that maybe the family should be left alone now. If nothing else, Noel's bloody nose was a sure sign that the family had some things to work out. Noel didn't stick around long after our fiasco either. Pride impelled him to get in his truck and drive himself home. His faggot brother had just decked him, after all. He really didn't need to stick around and have all his buddies from town witness the results.

Olive sent him off and assured him she would be home shortly; she wanted to help with the cleanup. It didn't take long anyway. The girls went through the house and picked up dirty plates, glasses, and coffee mugs. My mother stood at the sink, washing whatever dirty dishes came her way. Frank took the trash out, Cass at his side, and I grabbed a broom and swept the floor. Austin sat at the table, sipping the last of his coffee, and patiently waited for his wife to complete her daughter-in-law duties.

His eyes caught mine as I swept past him with the broom. "So, what happened down there?" he wanted to know.

"Nothing that hasn't been brewing for years," I said, shrugging. "Noel's had that coming for a long time."

"You two never did get along."

I smiled ruefully. *That* was an understatement. It didn't escape me that the girls were listening to our conversation as they puttered away in the kitchen. "Yeah, you're right. I guess we never did. Even when we were kids."

Frank came in then, fresh snow clinging to his suit coat and Cass's fur. "Well, I guess I should get goin'. It's startin' to snow again. Be good to get home before dark…"

We all looked at him, me especially. I didn't want him to go. I mean, I *really* didn't want him to go. There was a pain in my heart and even in my gut at the thought of watching his half-ton drive off the yard, leaving me alone in all this.

"Well, it was nice to meet you," said my mother, drying her hands on the dishtowel hanging on the oven door. "It was good of you to come down here."

My mother has always had this way of being polite and incredibly rude at the same time. I could hear it in the way she didn't say his name when she spoke to him and in the way she didn't ask him to stay.

"Probably got lots of chores to do at home," Austin said, "what with all those animals you told us about."

"Oh, I ain't too worried about that," answered Frank. "The neighbours can take care of 'em, if need be. They're really good that way. We help each other out a lot. No, it's more the roads I'm thinkin' of."

"Maybe you should just stay the night then," offered either Coral or Olive, I can't remember which.

"Oh, I don't know," he replied, his eyes on mine, trying to read my thoughts.

There were a few seconds of silence then, as if they were all waiting for me to speak. As if it were up to me.

"Yes," I said, "That's a good idea. You should stay here tonight."

And so that's what he did.

A little later we said goodbye to Austin, Coral, Olive, and my nieces and nephew. With the house once again tidy, I sensed my mother needed to be alone for a bit. Well, who could blame her, really? She'd lost her husband only days before and been bombarded by company ever since. Who could blame the woman for wanting some down-time now? Time to herself, time to reflect and plan. So I asked Frank if he'd like to go for a little drive to see my hometown. He thought that was a great idea.

And so we drove around town. There wasn't much to see; the school I attended, a few stores, town hall. Didn't take long at all. If it had been warmer, I guess we could have gotten out of his truck and walked around a bit, but there was a real chill in the air. I wasn't yet prepared to go back to the farm, so I suggested we stop in at one of the two restaurants and have a little something to eat.

So we did that. We pulled in front of the Wagon Wheel Café and got more than a little stared at by some of the community members there for supper when we strolled in. I guess we were quite a pair; an obvious city guy and a swaggering cowpoke. Though I didn't recognize them all, I'm sure many of the restaurant patrons knew I was *that* Hill brother. My brothers and I did kind of resemble each other, and I'm sure everyone around knew I was in town for my father's funeral. People do talk, after all.

We ignored the gawking and found ourselves a little corner booth. The place was decorated quite nicely, actually; very country-kitsch. Not my personal favourite, but appropriate décor for a place like this. Landscape prints hung on the walls and folk-art wooden cut-outs of chickens, roosters and cows perched on ledges. Hanging plants cascaded from the ceiling and wagon wheels had been propped against the wallboard.

A high school girl clad in blue jeans and a tight T-shirt poured us coffee, brought menus and took our order a few minutes later. I wasn't really hungry. I'd been snacking at Mom's all afternoon. Frank, on the other hand, was nearly ravenous. He'd been so busy at the house charming the ladies and impressing the hell out of the men with his knowledge of rural strife and hockey playoffs, that he really hadn't taken the time to eat anything. The waitress thought it was funny when he ordered a loaded buffalo burger and fries, while all I asked for was a bowl of soup.

I was dying for a cigarette more than anything but wasn't about to give in. I'd actually quit years ago. It was only a few days earlier, with the shock of Dad's passing, I had taken up the habit again. My craving must have been obvious because it was the first thing Frank said to me after we watched the waitress sprint away.

"Itchin' for a smoke?"

I'd been half listening to the song playing over the speakers. "Lost Together." A classic by Blue Rodeo. "No, I'm good," I half-lied. "How are *you* doin'? You sure you don't mind spending the night at my mother's?"

"No, it's all right, Jack," he answered. "I'll have to head back in the morning, though. The dogs and horses will be wondering where I am."

"Are they really going to be okay?" I looked out the window. The sun hadn't set so much as disappeared and it was getting dark.

"They'll be fine. The dog house is heated. And I phoned my neighbour from your mom's place. They'll swing by and check on everything."

We exchanged a few words about the day and the funeral, then he just blurted it out. "So why'd you punch your brother?"

"Because he's an asshole."

Frank chuckled. Actually, we both did. We were laughing pretty hard when the waitress came back and set down Frank's burger and my cabbage borscht. We settled back into conversation as we began eating.

"You don't like comin' down here, do ya?" he asked.

"Is it that obvious?"

"What don't you like about it?"

I was trying to formulate an answer as I sipped my soup, which tasted mighty fine. It was then I heard a female voice.

"Jackson Hill, is that you?"

I looked up to see who was speaking. She looked familiar, but I couldn't quite place her. I hadn't lived here in over twenty years, after all.

My bewilderment must have been plain because she identified herself as she perched on the bench beside me. "It's me," she squealed, "Roxanne Krochuk. Billy's sister. Oh, don't tell me you don't remember me? I know high school was twenty years and forty pounds ago, but it seems like only yesterday."

It all came back to me as I stared at the effervescent, big-boned redhead in her floral print dress and bright green coat. I had to stifle an outright chuckle when she made herself comfortable and leaned over to talk to Frank without even being introduced to him. Did the man have that effect on everyone?

"My younger brother Billy used to play in a local band with Jacky here," she said, her smile widening. "Him and his friend, and his sister-in-law, Coral.

Oh, I mean she wasn't his sister-in-law at the time. She was only dating his brother back then."

Her hands flew as she enthusiastically shared the story with Frank, who quirked an eyebrow at me in amusement before turning back to listen to her.

"Anyway, they were really great. The four of them. Oh, the school and the whole town just loved them. Jacky and his friend on guitar and Billy on drums, and Coral singing."

"Is that right?" Frank said with a grin of his own.

Unaccountably, I found myself blushing.

"Oh, yes! They were *fabulous*," she gushed. "Those were the days, weren't they, Jacky?"

"Those were the days," I repeated solemnly, sipping my soup.

"Oh, Jacky, where're my manners?" she asked then. "I was so sorry to hear about your father! Such a shame, such a loss. I wanted to come to the funeral this morning but I had to work. At the clothing store next door, you know? That's why I'm here. I'm just grabbing some take-out for supper. Joe doesn't like to cook. That's my husband. I married Joe Levinski. Oh, but maybe you know that already?"

"No, I didn't know," I said.

"Oh, yes, we've been married for years," she declared.

She stayed for several more minutes, telling us her whole life story as she waited for the waitress to bring her order; a lot more than either of us wanted or needed to hear. Frank amazed me, though, nodding and grinning as he ate, as if this strange woman hadn't interrupted or imposed at all. Finally, the girl brought Roxanne a big, greasy, brown paper bag packed full of food and she said her goodbyes and was off.

I have to say it was quite a relief to see her heavy-set butt go out the door.

"Ain't she a piece of work?" Frank winked, grinning that sexy mischievous grin of his.

"Isn't she just?" I affirmed.

He finished his burger contemplatively. "So, what'd ya guys call yerselves?"

"What do you mean?"

"Yer band in high school. The one she was talkin' about. What'd ya call yerselves?"

"Oh, we really didn't have a name," I said, setting my soup bowl to the side of the table. "We were just getting to the point where we were actually getting good enough that people wanted us to play at their events. You know, the usual stuff. Graduations and weddings and that. We were just getting to the point where it was all coming together when…"

I lost the words and my voice trailed off.

I waited a few moments for Frank to ask me something else, but he didn't. He didn't say anything. He just sat there, handsome in the black suit he'd worn all day. Just sat there across the table, with a soft smile and that comforting gaze of his.

FORTUNATE SON

IT ENDED UP being quite late when we returned to the farm. We went to the grocery store after we ate. Frank wanted a few things: a disposable razor, a toothbrush, deodorant. It was completely dark by the time we pulled into my parents' driveway.

Once again, I marvelled at what tranquil beauty the farm held, the old character home and barn serene beneath the blanket of new fallen snow. The dim light shining through the living room window told me my mother was still up, even though it was so late. Perhaps she was waiting up for me. It was kind of like going back in time.

Frank and I quietly walked into the house. Mom had changed into a nightgown and housecoat and was sitting in her rocking chair, while Cassie lay crashed-out on the couch, giving me the evil eye for abandoning her.

Mom looked up from the afghan she was crocheting. "Oh, you're back."

"Yeah," I said. "You must be tired. It's been a long day."

She nodded, removing her glasses. "Did you guys have supper?"

"Yeah, we did," I replied. "We stopped at the Wagon Wheel."

Frank and I sat on opposite ends of the couch, Cass sprawled out between us. I thought it strange, how we all left Dad's easy chair empty. It was as if he might come strolling into the house any minute and sit down in it, home from a town meeting or a curling game.

"Oh, you shouldn't have gone there. You should've gone to Fern's, beside the gas station. The food there is much better," she said with a weak smile. "But how were you to know? You hardly ever come down here." She yawned.

"Did *you* eat something?" I asked, rubbing my forehead, almost too worn out to make conversation.

"Oh, I made myself a bun," she said, quietly. "I fed the dog and took her outside too."

I nodded my thanks.

"So how come that is, anyway?"

"What?"

"How come you never come down here?" The words were blunt. "You avoid this place like the plague. Why are you so distant, Jack?"

Obviously the question had been weighing on her for some time. I could tell by the way she blurted it out, like she really needed to know. I looked from her down to the floor, unsure how to answer.

Frank stood then, stifling a yawn. "Well, if you all don't mind, I think I'll turn in. I'm pretty wiped." Clearly he felt the need to escape before the conversation became overly emotional.

"Oh! I've fixed up the room across the hallway from Jack's," my mother said. "There's fresh sheets on the bed and I set some towels on top of the comforter in case you'd like to shower."

"That's mighty nice of you," Frank smiled at her. "I'll see ya in the morning."

I watched his gentle swagger as he went up the stairs and disappeared into the darkness of the upper level. I didn't want him to go. Or rather, I wanted to go with him. I wanted only to curl up beside him again. To feel his skin. To smell his scent and listen to his soft snoring.

The crochet hooks were a blur in Mom's hands as she waited for me to speak.

"You know how busy I am," I said finally. "It's difficult to get away. It really is, when a guy owns a business and a house."

"I suppose," she said, not looking up, staring down at the afghan in the dimly-lit room.

There were a few moments of silence, the only sound that of water running upstairs; Frank must have taken her up on the shower.

She spoke again. "I just don't see why you had to do that. I don't see why you had to hit your brother. At your father's funeral, no less." She looked up then, dismay and resentment in her eyes.

"He was asking for it," I said, trying to keep calm. "He was pushing my buttons. You should have heard the shit he was saying to me."

Cassie lifted her head, picking up on my defensive tone.

"I did hear it," she retorted. "*Several* people heard it. They heard it all."

"I don't care," I half-mumbled.

"What?"

"I said, 'I don't care.'"

"Well, no, I suppose you don't. You're not the one who has to live in this town."

I couldn't help raising my voice.

"Oh, yes, of course!" I spit out. "*That's* what this all boils down to, after all. Keeping up appearances. As if we're perfect people in a perfect family, running a perfect farm. No *wonder* I never fit in around here, 'cause I sure as hell ain't perfect! Not like your other two sons. Such hardworking, God-fearing men. Great farmers, great husbands, great fathers, great sons! Well, they might as well be sainted. Noel especially!"

Mom stared at me for several moments, stunned and speechless.

"Look, Mom," I said, in control of my emotions once more. "I'm sorry for all this. I'm sorry Dad died. I'm sorry you have to watch your sons fight. And I'm especially sorry for embarrassing you at Dad's funeral. But I am who I am and that's all there is to it." I paused. "Do you really wanna know why I never come down here?"

She stared at me.

"Do you wanna know?"

"All right." She put down the crocheting. She looked unsure and I nearly relented, but this had been bottled up too deep, too long.

"I hate it," I said, my words low and furious. "I hate it all. The politics, the bullshit. Noel always trying to outdo everyone. You always making me feel like a piece of crap."

"And just how do I do that?" she asked, looking into my face.

I let out a huge sigh. "Look," I said. "I don't feel like I belong in this family. I never have and I obviously never will. You think I'm a loser and I've actually made a sort of peace with that. You think that because I didn't marry some local girl and settle down and become a farmer like my brothers, somehow that makes me inferior."

She leaned forward in her chair, shock clear in her expression. "Jacky, I'm sorry you feel the way you do, but I can assure you, I don't love any of my sons any more or any less than the rest. It's just…I simply don't understand everything you've done with your life."

I nodded, a painful smile curving my lips as I blinked back a sudden well of tears. "Ah, yes," I said. "That's what this is about, isn't it? That *really* what it's about after all these years."

"What?"

"This! What's been happening here today. The fact that Frank showed up. The fact that I was so glad to see him. The fact that he's a *man*. And he really is, Mother. Trust me, I've seen him naked."

I was deliberately harsh. Maybe I was even being mean, but I didn't care.

"Jackson, you live your life the way you choose and I don't say much…"

"The way I *choose?*" I stood up. "The way I *am*, Mother. This is *me*, this is who I am!"

She rubbed her eyes, the afghan slipping to the floor, unnoticed. She was completely exhausted and exasperated. "Oh, Jacky, I don't know. I don't know about any of this. You—you seem so angry about so many things. And one thing I know is that there comes a time when a person has to make peace with his hostility."

She rose from her chair and looked around—at me, at Cass, at the room. "If I were to get upset over every bad hand I've been dealt, I'd have such a rage…! Listen, Jackson, what I *do* know is that I'm way too tired to be having this conversation with you."

And with that she brushed past me and went into her bedroom, closing the door quietly but firmly behind her.

I sat back down and stayed there for quite a while, pondering it all; the entire day, our conversation. Finally, I dragged my tired body slowly up the stairs. But after a half-hour of tossing and turning, I found myself throwing back the down covers and stumbling across the hallway, Cass at my heels.

And when I stood in the doorway of the bedroom where Frank slept and saw him there, dark hair against the white pillowcase, I breathed in the deep peace of his dreamless slumber and knew I was doing what was right for me.

I rested my head on his chest and held him close, at last giving myself up to sleep.

SWEET EMOTION

I AWOKE LATER than expected in Frank's bed. It was Noel's old bed, actually. Definitely one of life's little ironies. Even though morning was well under way, it was still quite dark outside. Dark in the room too. Not so dark, however, that I couldn't help noticing Frank was nowhere to be found. I crawled out of the warm covers and stood looking out the bedroom window, still clad in the T-shirt and boxer shorts I'd slept in.

There were no vehicles in the yard other than my Volkswagen and Frank's blue half-ton. That told me one thing for certain: Austin and Coral, and Noel and Olive weren't here. Which meant Frank and my mother were probably downstairs alone together. The thought made me nervous, and I hustled to get my ass down there. I threw on a pair of jeans and after a quick pit-stop in the bathroom, I headed down the stairs. There they were, the three of them, settled in the dining room, Mom and Frank sitting at opposite ends of the oak table with Cass stretched out on the hardwood underneath.

To my surprise, they were so heavily engaged in conversation, neither one heard me coming down the stairs.

"'Morning," I said, interrupting them.

"Good morning," they replied, almost in unison.

I grabbed a mug from the cupboard and poured myself a coffee.

"I'm just going take Cassie outside and have a smoke, then I'll join you," I said, putting cream and way too much sugar into my mug.

"You can have a cigarette in here," Mom offered.

"That's okay; I'll go outside," I told her, throwing on my coat.

"I'll go out with you," Frank said, finishing the last of his toast. "I could use a breath of fresh air myself." He grabbed his jacket from the front closet and followed me out.

The weather wasn't bad. There was snow falling and no wind. A real stillness hung in the air; just blankets and blankets of white underneath the grey sky.

"How'd ya sleep?" asked Frank, a gleam in his eye.

I took a huge sip of coffee, followed by a long drag of my smoke.

"Actually, pretty good," I replied. "All things considered."

"Me too," he smiled, "It was nice of you to come and join me," he added, almost shyly.

"It *was* nice," I said, meeting his eyes. And it *had* been nice. The obvious connection we had was very nice indeed. "I can't believe how fast you fell asleep last night. Didn't you hear us arguing?"

"No. Why, what were you arguing about?"

I sipped my coffee, reflecting for a moment. "Nothing, really. Nothing and everything."

He laughed that contagious laugh. "She's not so bad, Jack. She's not so bad at all. In fact, I got one just like her."

"You make her sound like one of your horses," I said.

We both laughed then, our amusement slowly fading into the still morning air as we watched Cass sniff the ground.

Frank finally spoke. "There's one thing I can't figure out."

"What's that?" I asked, tossing my cigarette butt into the snow, and jamming my hands into my pockets.

"You said you guys never had animals when you were growing up."

"We didn't."

"Then why did your dad have that big red barn?" He pointed at it.

"Oh, we used it for storage," I said. "Grain, equipment—that kind of stuff.

Besides, I think when my parents built this place, Dad had planned on having livestock."

"So why didn't he?"

"Mom wouldn't hear of it. Austin said she was adamant. Said she didn't want anything to do with butchering or milking cows or gathering eggs. Said she just flat out refused to get into it all."

"That right?" Frank said. "And my mom was just the opposite. She loved being outside with the animals. That was her thing. Tending to her garden and her critters. The only reason she stopped was because she got too old and frail to take care of it all."

"Well, my mom's one of a kind." It was hard not to inject the words with sarcasm.

"You should take me on a tour," he suggested.

"Really?"

"Yeah, I'm funny that way. I like looking at other people's barns and such."

I chuckled but gamely led him across the snow-covered yard.

I was sure Mom was watching from the window of the house, curious as to what the hell we were up to. We opened the barn's double doors and I flicked on the lights. A flood of memories washed over me as the interior came into view. At one point in my life, I had spent a great deal of time in this barn. There were always so many chores that needed to be done when we were all kids. And it was out here I'd practised my guitar, away from everyone else in the family.

It was all just how I remembered it. The back half filled with stalls where horses—had we had any—might have rested. Dad had always used the stalls to store grain. The front half was a big, half-empty room. I think it was meant to serve as a storage area for hay bales and that sort of thing, for feed and supplies you would need to have around for livestock, but we had always used it for storage of other things. Judging by the looks of the place, it was still being used for storage. Dad's riding mower, a push mower, and some summer lawn ornaments had all been discarded in here.

"Well, this is it," I said, my hands outstretched in "ta-da" fashion.

"Oh, this is nice," he said, looking around. "Bigger than my barn. Your dad make those?" he asked, pointing to the pile of homemade lawn ornaments in the corner; wooden jackrabbits, squirrels, and skunks.

"Yeah, he did," I nodded. "Dad was pretty handy. He liked to putter out in the garage when he didn't have any other work that needed doing. He liked to keep busy."

"Like his son," he said, grabbing my hand, enjoying this time alone we were having. "What'd you use the loft for?" he asked, motioning to a paint-chipped ladder leading to a trapdoor.

"Oh, various things," I answered. "More storage. But when we were all kids we used to play up there a lot. In the summer we'd build a big pile of straw in front of the barn, then jump into it from the loft."

He grinned at me and I could feel myself blush under his gaze.

"Well, you know what it's like. It got boring at times. We were always coming up with things to do. Then, when we got older and my parents got new living room furniture, well, we boys all got smart and hauled their old stuff up there. It was kind of like our clubhouse. We used to go there to get away. We'd drink beer, smoke cigarettes or weed, and hang out. Austin and Noel used to haul their girlfriends up there too, in hopes of scoring."

"Coral and Olive?"

"Eventually. But there were others before that."

"And did they score?" he asked, leading me toward the ladder.

"Oh, I'm pretty sure they did," I replied.

"And you?"

"Yeah," I said, mildly embarrassed. "Me too."

"Come on, you can show me," he said, heading up the ladder, testing each rung to be sure it would hold.

I followed him up. I found it amusing. I'd never seen anyone get so excited about a barn. I have to say I was quite surprised when I reached the top of the rungs. The furniture my parents hadn't wanted was all still there, right where we'd left it when we hauled it up from the old farm truck and through the loft door: a tacky chocolate-brown chesterfield with hideous orange and yellow flowers, an easy chair to match, a beat-up dark-oak coffee table, a magazine rack, a tall chrome ashtray, complete with stinking, rotting cigarette butts. It was all as it had been the last time I'd been up here all those years ago.

Memories overcame me. Overwhelmed me too.

"Well, look at all this," Frank was saying, already ahead of me. "It's just like you described, complete with magazines in the rack." He held them up and waved them at me; my old *Rolling Stone* and *Spin* magazines and my brother's *Playboys* and car magazines.

Here I was in my favourite childhood hangout with this hunk of a man I still wasn't quite sure what to make of; it was all just a little strange. Nostalgic and exciting at the same time.

I followed Frank over to the couch. He smacked dust from the cushions and I set my empty mug down on the coffee table. I could hear Cassie whimpering from the lower level.

"Just stay put, Cass. We'll be down in a few minutes," I called down to her. I knew all she needed was to hear my voice; that's all she wanted. Just to know I was all right up here.

I turned my attention back to Frank, who had stretched out on the old couch. He was wearing the cowboy boots, suit pants and white dress shirt he'd been wearing when he drove down the day before. The tie and suit jacket were gone, replaced by a brown buckskin coat. I have to say, he looked mighty fine. I suspected he would no matter what he wore—or didn't. Now, though, he reminded me of nothing so much as the cover of a country and western album or an ad for Marlborough cigarettes.

"You're gonna get your dress clothes all dirty," I said. "It's pretty dusty up here."

"It's all right," he drawled. "Everything's washable."

It was then I realized that part of what drew me toward him was his ability to be completely easygoing. To just hang loose in any situation.

"You're right, it *is* kind of nice up here," he said. "Peaceful."

"I used to have a lot of fun up here," I told him, dusting a seat then leaning back in the chair. "Lots of laughs."

"With your brothers?"

"Sometimes. But friends too. I learned how to play guitar up here."

"From Anwar?" he asked.

It was odd to hear that name on his lips. Even though I'd thought of Anwar a lot over the years, it had only been in these last few days I had actually talked with anyone about him. Most of my friends in the city didn't even know he'd existed.

"Yeah," I said, my mind wandering into the past.

"What else did he teach you?" he prodded gently.

"What do you mean?" I asked, my palms sweaty now, my stomach heavy.

"You were lovers, weren't you?"

And just like that I just started to cry. Sitting there in that filthy, dilapidated chair in front of a man I'd met only a few days before, I just let out a waterfall of tears.

"Yeah," I said in a whisper. "We were."

"It's all right to cry, Jack," he sat up, leaning over to put a hand on my knee. "It's sort of a cleansing thing. I mean, in the last few days, you lost your father, decked your brother, and had an argument with your mom. Definitely not one of yer better weeks, right?"

I laughed out loud through the tears.

He smiled and his eyes were steady on mine. "Jackson, come over here."

I got up. I'm sure I was a real mess. I hadn't yet shaven or even washed my face, which was now stained with tears. I still wore the old T-shirt I'd slept in the night before, and the jeans I'd pulled on when I woke up were stained with coffee from the road trip. To top it off, I'm sure my winter jacket smelled of smoke. But none of that stopped Frank from scooping me into his muscular arms.

"I know you're hurting, Jack," he said. "But you know sometimes it's really good to talk about things—especially if you've got a willing listener."

And so, for the first time ever, I shared my memories of Anwar.

LIFE IN A NORTHERN TOWN

ANWAR AND I had a rare connection. We became fast friends when he transferred to our school in freshman year. The fact that I was far from being the most popular kid in class and that he was the new kid in town helped, I'm sure. It wasn't like either of us had gaggles of other friends we could hang out with. But even if we had, I'm positive we still would have been drawn to each other.

Anwar brought his guitar to school for the first few days. Then one morning, he suddenly stopped. Being kind of a shy boy, it took me the better part of the first break to ask him why he had left it at home. When I did, he replied simply that he had expected the school to have some kind of band or musical program, but when he had finally investigated and found out there were none, he saw no reason to keep lugging the guitar to school. He seemed disgusted by the situation and the school and the fact that small town schools didn't offer near the extracurricular activities he had grown accustomed to in the city where he'd lived before.

Anwar and I were both social outcasts, lovers of books and reading and art and music. In fact, that was what really bonded us. It made us soulmates. I'll never forget the look on his face one sunny afternoon as we ate lunch on the school lawn. I had asked, with some trepidation, if he could find the time and the patience to give me guitar lessons. I shouldn't have worried.

He thought it was a great idea.

It wasn't long before I'd saved up enough to buy my own guitar and found myself over at Anwar's practically every day after school to practise. Often Austin or Noel would have to drive back into town just before supper to pick me up and bring me home. Most times, they were upset with me for not being around to help do the many after-school chores that needed doing.

But I didn't care that they were mad. I didn't care that I wasn't doing my share of the work at home. I wouldn't even have cared if I had missed supper with my family. I was with Anwar and that was all that seemed to matter. I was learning to play guitar. I was learning about life and experiencing the world vicariously through him. He *became* my world. He helped me understand so many things about life and about myself; all those mixed-up feelings that had been churning around inside me for so long. He helped put everything in perspective.

I loved him for it. I loved him for so many things: his charm, his talent, his dark handsome face. I just loved him. Really deeply loved him.

Anwar had gotten his driver's license by the middle of the second semester of our sophomore year, and he would often give me a ride home in his father's car when school was done for the day. Having a mother who had somewhat of a short fuse in those years, and a father who always seemed to have an endless list of chores he wanted me to do, we would escape as often as we could to the loft in the barn. We would plunk ourselves down on this garish, discarded couch and practise our music for as long as we could get away with. And when we grew weary of strumming, we would talk and tell stories and secrets and jokes. We basked in each other's company, Anwar telling of his childhood in India and the city his family had emigrated to afterwards. I, in turn, told him of my dream of leaving the farm one day.

We planned our lives as professional musicians, dreamed of becoming stars. We fantasized about one day sharing a stage with our constantly growing list of idols: Leonard Cohen, Bob Dylan, Bono and Sting. We chuckled about how our audiences would be filled with screaming, love-struck girls with no clue about our secret relationship.

Oh, how we dreamed. How we laughed.

That's what we were doing one late spring afternoon, a Saturday when no one else was supposed to have been on the farm. Mom and Dad had driven into the city to buy groceries and pick up supplies. Austin and Coral were at a softball tournament in town. And Noel and Olive were supposed to have been at the tournament too. Turned out they'd felt the rush of spring fever just as we had, and decided to sneak home for a bit.

Anwar and I were lost in each other's arms on the chesterfield, just enjoying spending the day alone together, when I saw Noel's head out of the corner of my eye. Just his head sticking up from the trapdoor over there. The look on his face was priceless.

"What the hell are you two doin'?!"

And that was that. Noel had a field day. He couldn't wait to tell Austin and everyone else—the whole family, the whole school, the whole town. Even back then he was a hot-head and a big mouth. It didn't much matter; he and I had never been overly close. We hadn't really even liked each other much. The fact that he turned out to be a raging homophobic didn't really alter our relationship.

Life didn't change. Anwar and I got harassed at school a bit, but it was nothing we couldn't handle. There was lots of name-calling. Months later, in our junior year, when Anwar ran for vice-president of the student council, all his campaign posters got vandalized. Jerry Doyle ran against him and filled the walls of the school with posters that read: "Vote for Jerry, he's no fairy." But it was all manageable, somehow.

One time, walking to Anwar's house after school, we got tackled by the Zazansky brothers. They were more than a little surprised when we fought back and kicked the shit out of them a bit. Eventually the people of the town began to find other things to get worked up over: pregnant teenage girls and boys growing dope in their mothers' vegetable gardens. All the usual small-town scandals.

Things at home didn't really change much. Mom was in complete denial and went off into her own little world as she often did. Austin, the pacifist, just kind of accepted it in his own quiet way. He was dating Coral by then, and even in those days, the two of them always seemed to have the ability to go with the flow. Noel was Noel, complete with snide remarks and sneering jeers and crude remarks about what an embarrassment I was to him, to the family, to his friends—his precious redneck, beer-swilling, snuff-chewing friends. It was ironic. *He* was the one who'd blabbed it all over the community, and yet he was the one who felt so humiliated.

But I didn't care.

And Dad? My father was as he always was. Forever the quiet one, calm, and contemplative; the strong silent type.

I never knew how he felt about it. Never could figure it out. At least not until one Sunday afternoon, late in the summer before my senior year of high school. It was pretty quiet around the farm that day. Austin had just married Coral and they'd already moved into their brand-new home up the road. Noel was out with Olive or his friends, I'm not sure. Mother was in the kitchen, baking fruit pies and canning endless quart-sealers of berries and rhubarb. I was in my room going through school supplies, attempting to figure out what I needed to get from town for the upcoming school year.

Dad appeared in the doorway of my bedroom, something he didn't often do in those days. He asked me if I'd like to join him to inspect the fields. In a couple short weeks, harvesting would be well under way. I told him I had way too much to do. He surprised me a bit when he insisted I should get out of the house and get some fresh air.

So there we were, the two of us, rumbling down the bumpy road in his army-green '56 Ford truck, past fields of wheat, barley, and oats. Dad had always sown a multitude of crops every season. He said it made for good farming business. I always figured he just liked the variety of it all. He loved a challenge too. Different grains had different needs. Some needed more irrigation, some less. Some more growing time than others.

Dad had planted flax that summer, for the first time ever. I have to admit, the air smelled sweet and alluring as he put the stick-shift in park beside the enticing, watery-blue field.

"Come on," he said to me, swinging open the truck door. "Let's go take a look."

We stepped through a carpet of tranquil, hazy-blue, stalks waving in the gentle wind.

Dad finally spoke, staring straight ahead. "Your last year of school now," he said.

"Yup," I replied. What more was there to say?

"And then what, Jacky? What you got planned?"

"Don't know yet," I shrugged.

I could smell the blossoms in the air, their fragrant smell tickling and tantalizing my nostrils.

"What about Anwar?" he asked.

I was surprised by the question. I mean, Dad had always been kind enough to Anwar but never overly so. He never asked about him or anything when he hadn't seen him for a while.

"I don't think he's decided either," I replied. "He'll probably go to university. Become a music major. It'd be a shame to have all that talent and just go nowhere with it."

A hint of autumn was in the air, but the sun still shone brightly.

Dad lifted the ball cap off his sweaty forehead and rubbed his eyes a bit. "Pretty, ain't it?"

"What?"

"Flax. I mean, all the grains have their own appeal, but this here stuff is very pretty."

"Yeah, I guess," I said.

He stopped walking then, just gazed out over the field.

"Like people," he said. "People are like that too. Everybody's got their own little somethin' to offer to the world. But every now and again comes along someone that's just a little different. Just as good as everyone else. Hell, maybe even better. Just different."

He turned and began walking back toward the truck.

I followed quickly behind. It was then I knew how he really felt about me, about Anwar, about everything.

CHANGES

FRANK WAS RIGHT, crying was a cleansing thing. Same with talking. Still it felt a bit weird, sitting in my father's barn loft on this crisp winter morning, telling a man I hardly knew about my dead gay teenage lover. And Frank was an intent listener. He wasn't just pretending; he hung on every word. I appreciated that about him. There was a minute of silence as he absorbed the story. It was a peaceful quiet. All I could hear was our breathing, a few snowbirds chirping outside the rotting boards of the loft, and Cassie down below, scratching on an old gunnysack, trying to make herself comfortable. And then I heard a vehicle pull into the yard. One of my brothers, no doubt.

I had broken away from Frank's embrace as I told my story. It was surprisingly warm up in the loft; the time had flown and it was now late morning. The weather had smartened up a bit too, after the moodiness and bluster of the last few days.

Frank had opened his jacket and I'd leaned back onto his chest. He stroked my uncombed hair.

"That's quite a story," he said. "Your father was obviously a hell of a man. The type not to judge a person."

"Yeah."

"'Never judge a man 'til you've walked a mile in his shoes.' Isn't that the expression?"

"Yup," I said softly, nuzzling into the soft white of his dress shirt; the shirt he had put on for me, to drive down here and give his support at this trying time. I felt tired again, like I could just sleep for a bit. I let myself be lulled into a quiet sort of daze as Frank stroked my hair, not really thinking about anything. We didn't hear the barn door open below, or the creak of the ladder as someone climbed it. And then we heard Coral's voice.

"*Here* you guys are! Grace is worried, Jack. She said you guys have been in here a long time." Coral was cheery as usual, her voice holding concern but no censure.

I sat up, pulling away from Frank. I'm not sure why, because there was no awkwardness and no reason to hide our connection or anything. It was just a natural reaction.

"Oh, I guess we got distracted," I said with a light laugh.

"I see that," she answered pertly, tossing back her dark hair. "Come up to the house when you're ready. We'll have coffee." She turned to descend the ladder.

"You don't hafta go," called Frank.

"Oh," she said, grinning her illuminating grin. "I thought maybe you wanted to be alone."

"I'm just reminiscing," I said. "Reliving the glory days."

Coral walked over and plopped down on the easy chair. "Oh, the glory days. I think about them often too." She seemed lost in thought for a minute, then went on. "But your mom's freaking out a bit. She wants to know what you're doing out here."

"I'll bet she does," I said. We all laughed.

"Jackson," Coral said, growing serious, glancing at Frank then back to me. "About what I said to you the other day when we were walking? I…I think I owe you an apology. I was kind of a mess there for a few days. I laid so much on you. There was just a lot going on, you know? I was just, well, overwhelmed, I guess."

She looked pretty that morning. Her silky brown hair hung loose behind her shoulders. Her bright yellow winter coat matched her sunny mood. Clean, tight blue jeans hugged her fit body.

"It's all right," I said. And it really was. "I think we've all been overwhelmed. It's been quite a bit to digest."

She nodded, sitting back and relaxing as she looked around. "I hadn't realized all this was still up here." She began flicking through the magazines like Frank and I had when we'd first come up into the loft. "*Penthouse,* eh? These were probably Noel's. Wouldn't have been my husband's," she said with a grin.

"Don't be so sure," I replied. "Everyone was young once. Even Austin."

"Hey, look at this," she said, holding up a copy of the *Western Producer.* "It only dates back to a few weeks ago. Wonder where it came from?"

She held it out for us to see. She was right; it was a recent copy.

"Well, whaddya know," I said. "*Someone's* been coming up here. This place wasn't as neglected as we thought."

"Wonder who?" Frank said idly.

Coral's mind shifted gears again. "You know, Jackson, what I said to you the other day? It wasn't just grief talking. I was serious about a lot of it."

"What do you mean?" I asked, pleased she was willing to open up in front of Frank; it meant a lot. And it seemed I wasn't the only one who found his presence a comfort.

She looked like she was dying to get some things off her chest. "You know, every morning I send the kids off to school and Austin off to work. Even in the off-season, it always seems he's got something he's got to do every day. Business to take care of. Errands to run."

She looked back and forth between us and right into our faces as she spoke. "You know, it gets boring out here at times. *Really* boring. I mean, a woman can only scrub her floors so many times. She can only dust so many knick-knacks. She can only bake so many batches of cookies…" She stopped and took a breath. "I woke up one morning a couple years ago and discovered I had no idea who I was or what I wanted out of life. Does that make sense to you guys?"

I nodded. It really did, I wasn't just trying to be empathetic.

"I need to get away from here," she continued. "If only for a while. I really need to get away from this town. Do you guys realize I've never lived any-where but here? Isn't that something? I've spent my whole life living right in the middle of nowhere. I need to know what it feels like to be somewhere else for a while. *Be* someone else. Someone other than the mother of the Hill twins or Austin Hill's wife, or even Olive Hill's sister."

"I can understand that," I said.

Frank just listened, a look of sympathy on his face.

"That's what I came here this morning to talk to you about," she said. "I need something from you, Jack."

"From me?"

She nodded. "In a few months—in the fall, actually—the twins will be going away to university. And when that happens, I…I want to come live with you, Jack. If only temporarily. I want to come stay in the city with you. How would you feel about that?"

"I think that'd be fine," I answered. It all sounded all right. I would have to give it some thought, but Coral and I had always gotten along very well.

"And I don't mean I'd be freeloading. I can take care of myself. I got money saved up. I got money Austin doesn't even know about. And besides all that, I'd get a job. I'm thinking about taking some classes too, but I can work as well," she said, leaning forward in the dusty chair. Her enthusiasm was compelling. "I have a few skills. I can clean, cook, take care of kids. I could waitress or something. I've helped out at Fern's Place in town, you know."

"You've obviously given this a lot of thought," I remarked.

She leaned back and laughed her spirited laugh. "Oh, I have, you guys. More than I even care to admit. So, what do you think?"

"I think it'd be fine. Austin would probably murder me, but it'd be fine," I said. "Still, autumn is months away. See how you feel when the time comes."

We heard another vehicle pull into the driveway then. I heard Cassie whimpering too. She was growing impatient.

"That's probably Olive," Coral surmised. "I told her to meet me here for coffee."

The three of us reluctantly came down to earth. It had been so relaxing in the loft. Such good company I had found myself in—yet I knew I had to come down and face the day. I also knew Frank had to be getting anxious to get on the road and go home.

We came out of the barn just as Olive went into the house. What a bright, clear day it was turning out to be. The sun almost blinded us as we strolled across the yard and followed her inside.

Frank ran upstairs to grab his suit coat. It was about the only thing he'd come out here with. He said a quick hello to Olive, thanked my mother for her hospitality and the two of us went back outside.

My mother muttered a cold "It was nice to meet you," as we closed the door.

I was grateful it was good travelling weather now. With the air clear and the road manageable, Frank would be all right.

We stood beside his big blue Silverado. I figured my sisters-in-law would be watching from the kitchen window, wondering how this was going to go. Would we hug? Would we kiss?

"You know," Frank said, "you could stop at my place. On yer way back, I mean. Stay at my farm for a couple days. When you goin' back, anyway?"

"Oh, probably tomorrow," I replied. "I got some things to take care of here yet."

"Then I'll see you tomorrow," he said, ruffling Cass's fur.

"Oh, I don't know," I said. "I got to get back to the city. I got things to care of there too."

"One more night away ain't gonna make that big a difference," he grinned.

"We'll see."

"You're not gonna make me beg now, are ya?"

I smiled back at him. "All right," I said. "I'll stop. You better tell me exactly where your farm is or I'll never find it."

"I'll do better than that," he said, completely enthused now. "I'll meet you in town. You let me know what time you're gonna be there, and I'll meet you in front of Ming's. You know, that Chinese café, you ate at? Hell, I'll even buy you supper. Then you can just follow me out to the farm. How does that sound?"

"Sounds good," I said. It did too.

He climbed into his truck. He leaned out to close the driver's side door, then stopped. "Oh, and Jackson," he said, "don't let it all get to ya."

"What do you mean?"

"The family. Whatever it is you gotta deal with here now. Don't let it get you down. Somehow everything just has a way of workin' out. You know what I mean? It'll all be all right in the end."

"I hope so," I said quietly. "Thanks for coming, Frank." I grabbed the truck door and began to close it.

"You're welcome."

And then I'm not sure who initiated it, but our eyes met for a fleeting second and then our lips in a soft, lingering kiss.

I could still feel the soft bristle of his mustache and the stubble of his chin as I watched his truck barrel down the road until it gradually disappeared from sight.

I had a quick cigarette. I felt I needed it—or deserved it, maybe. My cowboy was gone and I'd been left to deal with Noel and my mother. I was subdued as I stepped back into the house.

Mom was standing at the kitchen counter, already preparing lunch. She had a pot of broth on the stove and was chopping and dicing vegetables with an intensity that made me wince. I'd forgotten how she liked to keep production going at all times.

Coral and Olive were perched at the table, sipping steaming cups of fresh coffee. They both gave me all-knowing grins as I poured myself one too.

"Is he gone?" Mom wanted to know.

"Yup, he's gone," I replied.

"You were in that barn a long time," she said, a tinge of aggravation in her voice as she sliced bread and cheddar cheese. "I don't know what it is about that barn. People go in there and they don't come out for what seems like forever. Even your father. When he used to go in there with his *Western Producer*, I always knew I wouldn't see him again for hours."

Coral and I exchanged a look.

I was secretly relieved when both my sisters-in-law hung around for a bit and joined Mom and me for lunch. We made light conversation over an equally light meal of leftovers from the day before.

Somewhere between the ham and cheese bunwich and the carrot cake, Olive talked me into going over to their house that evening for supper. I had a bad feeling about it but still couldn't say no to her, especially since she seemed so excited about it. She and Coral pulled on their boots and coats, discussing the menu as they did.

And later, when they were gone, after I'd helped Mom with the cleanup and persuaded her to lie down for a nap, I took Cassie for a walk, strolling down the snow-laden gravel road. I took a good long look at the frosty fields surrounding me, thinking of my dad. He'd loved this land, maybe even more than his own family. I stopped walking to properly inhale the beauty and peace of it all, the tranquility and the wide open sky nearly overwhelming me.

A good couple minutes went by and I was smiling through tears at Cassie's bewildered expression. She couldn't figure out why we'd stopped walking, not understanding I'd had an epiphany.

I wondered what my brothers would think.

GRACELAND

OH, OLIVE, WHY DID I allow you to talk me into this? I was feeling some really bad karma. Mom and I were crammed into my tiny car, letting it properly warm up before heading over to Noel and Olive's for supper and I was kicking myself real hard now. Olive claimed she loved to cook and since her kids were now older and off having lives of their own, it seemed she never had much opportunity to exercise her culinary skills. But I still couldn't help thinking how awkward this dinner party would be, given recent events. Sitting across the supper table from Noel and his great big shiner would be real uncomfortable for everyone.

So it was with severe apprehension I'd opened the passenger door of the car for my mother and looked back at Cassie staring at me through the kitchen window, completely annoyed with me for leaving her behind again.

"Not a very big car," Mom observed as we pulled out of the driveway and onto the icy road.

"Well, I don't need much," I said. "Not like my brothers. I'm sure they need those great big vehicles for hauling stuff around and all that." I silently made a pledge to myself to be on my best behaviour for the evening and just let everything roll off me. To be more like Frank.

She looked around the car: the coconut-scented air freshener hanging from the rear view mirror, the empty take-out coffee cups littered across the floor, the ashtray half-filled with cigarette butts.

"I thought you quit smoking," she said.

"I did," I told her.

"Oh."

We rode in silence for a few moments. "Oh, you brought your guitar," she said, glancing into the back seat.

"Yeah."

"What for?"

"Oh, I don't know. Just in case, I guess. Thought I might play a tune or two at the funeral."

"Why didn't you?"

"You didn't ask me."

"Oh."

Before I knew it, we were passing Austin's. There were no vehicles in the darkened yard. They must have left already. They were, after all, to meet us for supper as well. Two more miles to Noel's.

"I don't think we should stay late," Mom said. "Everybody's so tired. I can't believe the planning involved in a funeral. Or the expense. It's like it's a crime to die or something."

"Are you sure you want to move, Mom?" I asked then. "Are you absolutely certain that's what you want to do? I mean, just because that's what Noel thinks is best for you doesn't mean that *is* what's best for you."

She had no time to respond. We were already pulling into the yard. It was only then that it occurred to me it had been years and years since I had been at either of my brothers' homes. I took Mom by the arm and guided her into the house. All the wet snow that had fallen made the sidewalk leading to the four-level-split extremely slippery. We'd had enough trauma in the family for the time being, there was no need for anyone to take a nasty fall.

Since we were expected I saw no reason to ring the doorbell and we both just quietly stepped into the house. I had completely forgotten how artistic Olive was. Not only did she have exquisite taste in clothing, she had amazing decorating skills. She had created a sort of zen atmosphere in her home. I guess living with Noel would make anyone long for serenity. My parents' house was comfortable and felt lived in, but Olive's was like something out of a lifestyle magazine.

My brothers sat on the cream-coloured leather couches in the living room, both of them in dark denim jeans and western-style shirts, each just emptying a bottle of beer. I helped Mom remove her coat and then took off my own. Coral walked out from the kitchen, drying her hands on a tea towel, while her sister poked her head around the corner.

"You're right on time," Olive said in a cordial tone. "And you both look great, by the way. You must have spent the afternoon getting some much-deserved rest."

I had, as a matter of fact. I'd gone up to my old bedroom and crashed for a couple of hours after my walk with Cass. Mom's nap seemed to have rejuvenated her a bit too.

"What can I get you to drink?" Olive continued. "I know Grace doesn't want anything, but what about you, Jacky? There's cold beer. And I just uncorked some of my wine."

"You make your own wine?" I asked.

"All the time," she laughed. "We make our own everything around here."

"Got any rum?" I asked.

"Sure do." She disappeared to fix me a drink.

Coral guided me into the living room, the towel still in her hand. It was as if she were chaperoning, like she felt she needed to keep an eye on things.

My mother made a beeline for the kitchen. I knew she would offer to assist with the meal. I also knew Olive would send her away, out to the living room. Olive was quite accustomed to multi-tasking. She enjoyed it too; preparing supper, setting the table, fixing cocktails, all while entertaining guests. It was obviously nothing new to her.

Olive's touches were everywhere in the room too. Sprawling sprays of dried flowers hung on the taupe-coloured walls. Olive had likely made them herself, more than likely with flowers right out of her garden.

"How are you guys?" I asked my siblings as I sat down on the leather easy chair. "Where are the kids?" I continued, looking around the room, inhaling the vanilla-scented tea-lights scattered throughout and eyeing the massive painting of a prairie landscape hanging behind the sofa. "Nice place," I added, taking my fresh rum and Coke complete with squeeze of lemon from Olive's hand and setting it on a coaster on the cherrywood coffee table.

"They're not really kids anymore, Jacky," said Austin. "The twins will be graduating this spring."

"So I hear," I said, flashing Coral a look as she rose to rejoin her sister in the kitchen. She seemed to think there was enough ease in the room that she could go back to lending a hand.

"And Noel's kids too," he added. "Brandon will be graduating with them. Then Emma the year after. We'll all be empty-nesters before you know it."

More than you know, Austin, I thought.

"Anyway," he continued. "We're practically empty-nesters right now. The twins are both playing hockey in town tonight. That's why they ain't joining us. Brandon too."

"What about Emma?" I asked, looking out the picture window to the dark, snow-filled lawn out front. It was snowing once again. At least Frank would be home by now. I didn't have to worry about him driving on weather-stricken highways.

For the first time since we'd come in, Noel spoke. "She's upstairs getting ready. Got a date. Got herself a boyfriend now."

"That's nice," I remarked.

"I guess."

Mom came into the living room and took a spot on the piano bench. She seemed apprehensive. Like she just wanted to escape all this. I could sympathize. She knew I was planning to go back to the city in the morning. She knew the four of us had things to discuss. We all knew it.

It was a relief when my niece bounded down the stairs. It kind of broke the uneasiness. Emma had grown into a lovely girl. She had Noel's fiery-red hair, and yet she was so different from him.

"Hi, Uncle Jacky," she said. "Hi, Grandma."

She was so precious standing there at the bottom of the stairs, giving herself a quick once-over in the full-length mirror that hung in the front hallway. Her young, shapely body was squeezed into a pair of khaki hip-huggers and a bright blue pullover. I marvelled at her—those poignant teenage years, those few precious years when a person can really wear whatever it is they please and perhaps even do whatever they please.

"You're going out in that?" Noel asked, his voice deepening in patriarchal concern. "That sweater doesn't even cover your midriff."

"Oh, Dad," she said, "it's mid*riff*, and I'll be wearing my coat anyway. We're only going to watch the hockey game." She smiled at her father and he backed down a bit.

"Emma, you better not be home too late," Olive called from the kitchen. "It's a school night, after all."

"How late is not too late?" Emma asked, going into the kitchen to negotiate curfew with her mother.

That left the four of us alone in the living room once again. We settled into safe conversation. Usual small-talk topics like current events, the weather, the new linoleum in the entryway.

I was reminded of my own youth on the farm a few minutes later when Emma's date pulled into the driveway and honked the horn of his father's truck and she sprinted out of the house to join him. I had a childish urge to go with her, to go into town and sit in the chilly hockey rink and lose myself in the recklessness of the game. But reality quickly set in.

"Supper's ready!" Olive called.

It was with deep reluctance that I rose from the comfy chair and took my place in the dining room.

COME TOGETHER

SUPPER ACTUALLY ENDED UP being surprisingly pleasant. It was delicious too, and I found myself enjoying sitting at Olive's impressive cherrywood table, listening to a compilation of Gordon Lightfoot hits on the CD player and savouring slow-roasted pork loin and crabapple sauce, oven-roasted potatoes, dilled baby carrots, and Cobb salad.

With the help of my lovely sisters-in-law, and a glass or two of homemade chokecherry wine, the conversation flowed lightly through the dining room as we shared the meal. Even Noel and I made a strained yet decent effort at conversation, steering clear of anything that might lead to a disagreement. I was determined that Olive's efforts for a nice evening would not be in vain. I owed her that much. Hell, I owed Dad that much too. Still, every time I glanced at my brother's shiner and swollen cheek, I couldn't help but giggle a bit inside.

"Well, that was one great meal," I sighed as I finished my last bite and threw the burgundy linen napkin onto my soiled plate. "The roast was done to perfection, Olive."

"Oh, it was probably so good because it was fresh. I just bought it from the Zazanskys down the road. They've been butchering," she replied.

I smiled. Life really was dramatically different out here.

"Really? Well, it was awesome. The whole meal was."

"Oh, well, it's not over yet," she stated as she stood to collect the dirty plates. "Coral brought dessert. And I've got a new coffee press I'm just dying to try out. But you should all go back in the living room and relax."

"I'll help you clean up," I offered, rising now too.

"Absolutely not," she said. "I've got the whole rest of the evening. Tomorrow too, as far as that goes. Go sit with your family, Jacky. In the morning, you'll be going back to the city and who knows when we'll see you again."

I followed my mom and my brothers back into the living room. Truth be told, I'd rather have been in the kitchen, scrubbing dirty pots and pans with the girls.

"One thing about my wife, she's a hell of a cook," Noel boasted as he settled into his favourite corner of the couch. He turned to me. "Bet you don't get meals like that in the city."

"No, you're right," I said honestly. "Lots of take-out. Lots of quick, easy meals. 7-Eleven has the best nachos."

He stared me up and down. I couldn't really think of anything more to talk about with him. All the safe topics had been exhausted and I wished Mom or Austin would say something, but no one did.

"So, what'd you decide?" Noel asked abruptly in that demanding tone of his. "Are you sellin' or what?"

I looked around. His words had made Mom instantly uptight, and Austin suddenly looked much older than he really was. I stared unseeing at the caramel-coloured walls for a minute. So tasteful when Noel was anything but.

"No," I said, and my voice was calm. "I'm not."

Noel laughed. It was the kind of artificial laugh when you know a person is trying, not very successfully, to hide his contempt and aggravation.

"You better think about that long and hard, little brother. You got any idea what you're gonna get yourself into, being one-third owner of this all?"

"Oh, I've thought about it," I said, keeping my voice even as I looked straight at him. "It was a quiet afternoon and I went for a long walk with Cass today. I thought about it a lot."

Silence filled the air then. It was a relief when Coral came in a few moments later and began handing out slices of the raspberry cheesecake she'd spent the afternoon making. She quickly went back to the kitchen to make coffee.

"Well, *that* kind of puts Austin and I in a bit of an awkward situation," Noel sneered as he began dug into his cheesecake, not waiting for either his wife or sister-in-law to join us. "I mean, farming is a hands-on operation, right? A family farm requires real teamwork. I don't see how you plan on bein' a partner while you're livin' up there in the big city. You know, when Dad was alive, he was always sole owner, but the three of us worked together—me and Austin and him. It was more than a full-time job for all of us. And now with our own kids all movin' away come fall, well, we ain't even gonna have *them* around to help out."

I set my dessert down on an end table. "So hire someone to help out in the busy seasons," I suggested. "There's always a lot of guys around here looking for extra work. Pay him out of my share of the profits. Keep it all fair."

"You got it all figured out, don'cha?" Noel muttered, setting his empty dessert plate on the coffee table in front of him with a loud clatter.

"Like I said, I had lots of time to think today."

Olive came into the living room with Coral then. She put a serving tray of fresh coffee, cream, sugar, and mugs down on the coffee table, and sat down beside her husband. Coral took a spot beside Mom. I was glad to see them. I wanted everyone to hear this conversation.

"It just ain't all that easy, you know?" he continued. "It's hard to find good workers. And when you do find one, he wants big money right away."

"Oh, don't I know it," I said, leaning back in the chair, not backing down. "I run a business too, remember. I know what it's like. Good help is hard to find."

Noel shot a foul look across the room at me. More silence. All that could be heard was Lightfoot's melodic voice over the stereo speakers. "Song for a Winter's Night."

"Well, I guess it's settled then," said Austin, trying to ease the tension.

Noel stood. His face was red enough to match his hair. "Now just a minute. Not so fast. I don't see why all our lives gotta get all screwed up now, just because you're in the mood to be difficult." He pointed a long leathery finger at me.

"I'm not trying to be difficult," I said, taking a cup of coffee from Olive's shaking hand. "I'm just following Dad's wishes. That's all. Nothing more. Nothing less."

"Whaddya mean?"

"Dad left the farm to the three of us. Obviously he had his reasons. Maybe he really believed there could be some unity among us. Some real teamwork. And if that was his final wish, well, who am I not to at least give it one hell of a try? I owe him that much. We all owe him that much."

Quiet filled the room then, as my family absorbed my words.

Not much more was said about it for the remainder of the evening. We finished our cheesecake and drank our coffee over safer topics once again, like the kids' plans and the music playing on the stereo.

And by ten, when I saw the fatigue in Mom's eyes, I knew it was time to head back. "Are you ready to go?" I asked her.

"Whenever you are, son," she answered.

That surprised me. She hadn't called me "son" in years. I got up to leave. "Well, thanks again for the lovely meal, Olive, but I think we're both ready for bed."

"I think we'll go too," said Coral, checking the clock. "You ready, Austin?"

He nodded. There was a bit of a jam in the front hall as we got our coats and found our boots. Noel didn't get up off the couch, not to give anyone a hand, not to say goodbye. He just sat there. Perhaps he was exhausted as well. Or perhaps he was merely drunk.

Either way, Austin and Coral headed out to their car. Mom followed and got into mine. I'd command-started the engine a few minutes before we'd got our coats on and the vehicle would be toasty warm inside by now. Coral waited inside their Ford Explorer while Austin brushed the snow off the windshields of both vehicles.

"I won't be by in the morning," Olive said, throwing her arms around me. "I hate goodbyes. Especially when it comes to certain people. You being one of them."

I hugged her back. I held her for a few moments longer than usual. She had gone all-out this evening and it meant a lot to me. *She* meant a lot to me. Such an incredible person. Anyone who could be married to Noel all these years was obviously one hell of a woman.

"I'd better get going," I said. "Mom's waiting."

"All right," she nodded, "but do me a favour. Don't wait another three years to visit."

I smiled. "You know, the road goes two ways. You all could come up my way too."

"Yeah, right! As if I could ever get your brother to go anywhere other than into town or onto his field," she replied with a laugh, closing the door behind me.

I walked out to the car, suddenly feeling badly for her. I knew there'd be a big mess in the kitchen waiting to be cleaned up. I knew Noel would still be sitting there too. He'd be planted in the living room for her to contend with, drunk and disappointed, as if everything were all about him.

HAPPY JACK

MOM WASN'T QUITE AS EXHAUSTED as I'd thought. Once I'd fed Cass the scraps of pork loin Olive had been careful to send back for her, and taken her outside to do whatever business she needed to do, I was mildly surprised to walk back into the darkened kitchen to find Mom standing at the counter, steeping a pot of tea.

"Can I pour you a cup? It's chamomile," she offered, adjusting the belt of her soft-pink terry cloth housecoat. "It'll help you sleep."

"I won't have any problem sleeping tonight," I said. "But I'll sit with you while you have yours, if you like."

She poured the steaming tea into a Royal Albert tea cup. "Let's go sit in the other room," she suggested.

I followed her into the living room and sat down on the side of the couch closest to her rocking chair.

"The evening went better than I expected," I commented.

"It was nice," she replied, like it would pain her to ever get too enthusiastic about anything.

Then she surprised me.

"I think what you did tonight was very good," she said softly, sipping her tea and staring out at the snow blustering outside the window.

"You do?"

She nodded. "Maybe you're right. Maybe your father had a plan. What was the word you used? Unity?"

"Yeah," I said, rubbing a very clingy Cass behind the ears. "You know, it really doesn't mean you have to move. Not if you don't want to. You could stay right here."

"I want to," she said.

"Really?"

She nodded again, and her eyes were melancholy. "It gets lonely out here, you know."

"I'm sure it does."

She seemed to be feeling out what to say as she spoke. "I just feel—isolated. Even before your father died. He was always off doing something. I've spent too much time alone here. It gets to a person. All alone in the middle of the prairie. Especially this time of year. On those coldest winter days when the wind is blowing full speed. Some days it's as if it just blows right through the whole house. Through me too."

She finally broke her stare out the window and turned to me. "Some days it's enough to chill me right to the bone." She rubbed her thin shoulders then picked up her tea, cradling the cup as if warming herself on the hot porcelain.

"You know, I've been meaning to give you something ever since you got here the other day. It's been so hectic." She went into her bedroom only to emerge a few moments later with a shoe box. "A couple years ago, I started going through things. The storage room, closets, that sort of thing. Every now and again I'd come across something you boys'd left behind."

She handed me the box. "I don't know if you want any of this or not, but it's all yours. Do whatever you like with it. I gave Austin and Noel their things months ago."

I took the box from her hand and set it on my lap. Cass nosed it in sleepy curiosity.

Mom took her empty cup into the kitchen and set it in the sink.

"Anyway, you'll have to excuse me now. I'm suddenly very tired. I think I need to turn in. See you in the morning." She didn't bother to close the bedroom door behind her this time.

"Goodnight," I spoke softly.

I didn't stay up much longer; I was weary myself. I shut off the only lamp that was on and went upstairs.

I felt like I could use a shower but was too tired to tackle even that. Instead I merely brushed my teeth, washed my face and stripped down to my shorts and the muscle shirt I had been wearing underneath my sweater. I considered calling Frank, but it was already late and I didn't feel right about waking him up, though I knew he wouldn't have minded.

I caught a glimpse of the shoe box on the dresser where I'd left it when I came upstairs. I picked it up, settling in with Cass on the bed. And in the dim circle of light cast by the lamp on the night table, I slowly removed the lid.

There wasn't much to see; Mom had been right. There was nothing I was really dying to keep. My old pencil case from high school, the lock from my locker, a tacky curling trophy. I read the plaque: Most Improved Player. Not best or greatest, but most improved. Oh, well, it was better than nothing. I shuffled through the box. There were a few old guitar picks and some cassette tapes. I smiled inwardly. Back before compact discs, cassettes were *it*. I read the band names: The Rolling Stones, Kiss, Lynyrd Skynyrd, stuff I would still enjoy listening to. I thought I'd keep the cassettes for pure nostalgia if for no other reason.

I was about to put the lid on the box and hit the hay when I saw them. A chill ran through me as I slowly reached inside and pulled out the two black-beaded bracelets. With more than just a couple of tears in my eyes, I sat back against the headboard and drifted into one of my favourite memories of Anwar.

It had been the Christmas break of our senior year of high school. Christmas Day, actually. The time had passed enjoyably enough. We had done all the usual family stuff. Mom and Dad and I had all risen early that morning, and Austin and Coral and the girls had come over soon after. Noel and Olive had just gotten married and spent the day as well. We'd opened stockings and presents, sharing laughs as we lounged over coffee and eggnog and Mom's famous cranberry muffins. After cleaning up the mountain of discarded gift-wrap and straightening up the living room, us guys played cards while the girls prepared the traditional huge dinner of turkey, stuffing, mashed potatoes and all the other fixings.

It was always the kind of meal where everyone just stretched out after. The guys lazed around the living room, belts undone, completely lethargic, discussing the tools they'd gotten from wives or kids and the ongoing hockey season. The girls sat as well, sipping coffee and eyeing the massive stack of dirty dishes, working up the energy to attack the labour ahead, preparing to submerge their hands into hot soapy water and scrub away at pots and pans, clean the kitchen, and find places in the cupboards and drawers for their own newly-acquired gifts.

We were all in this state when Anwar drove down the snow-laden driveway in his father's car. Mom had been sitting at the kitchen table with the girls and called into the living room that he had arrived. I met him at the door, and after he exchanged holiday greetings with my family, I led him up to my room, anxious to give him his Christmas gift and not about to wait a moment longer.

"How was your morning?" I asked as I closed the bedroom door behind us.

"Good," he answered, flopping down on my bed as he usually did. "I can't stay long. My mom said I could only have the car for a little while. She wants me back at the house. 'Christmas only comes once a year,' and she wants the family together. She was pissed off last night. Dad had to run in to the hospital."

"Anything serious?" I asked, turning to him from the dresser where I'd been retrieving his gift from the top drawer.

"No," he replied, his face breaking into a grin. "A bunch of kids were playing hockey on Krochuks' pond. One of the Zazansky boys got hit in the face with a stick." He laughed out loud. "By his own brother! They were even playing on the same team. Showin' off, I guess, acting like a big pro and high-sticking all over the place. And then his brother wasn't watching where he was going and skated right into his stick. Cut his lip all to shit. Needed a bunch of stitches."

"That's hilarious," I said, taking out the carefully wrapped package.

"Sure is. Serves the assholes right."

"Well...Merry Christmas," I said, handing it to him.

"Oh, wow. Thanks, Jack." His hand was warm where it brushed against mine as he took it from my hands. "You didn't have to get me anything. I know you can't really afford it."

I shrugged this off.

"Dad paid me a bunch of money for helping with harvest this fall. It's really no big deal."

"Well, thanks anyway," he said, tearing open the candy cane paper.

The look on his face said it all. I knew he was thrilled. It was a different time then; compact disc players were just working their way into peoples' homes. I knew his parents had recently purchased one. It seemed only natural that CDs would be the perfect gift.

His face lit up as he sifted through the three I'd given him. I still remember what they were: The Eagles' *Hotel California*, Fleetwood Mac's infamous *Rumors* album, and *Synchronicity* by The Police, a real variety to start his collection.

"Oh, man! What I got you isn't this impressive," he said shyly.

"It doesn't matter," I said. And I meant it. It *didn't* matter. I was deeply in love. Anwar was all the gift I needed.

He reached into the front pocket of his jeans, slowly bringing out two beaded bracelets that looked exactly like the two he always wore on his wrist. He held them in front of him, between us, reaching for my right hand.

"These bracelets," he said, "they're like a family thing where I come from. We all wear them." He rested my forearm on his lap. "My brother and sister wear them; my parents wear them. Even my aunts and uncles back home. They're like a bonding thing." He looped one bracelet around the other as he spoke. "It's symbolic, you know? It just means that no matter where we all are, no matter what we all do, we're still together in a way." He slid the bracelets over my hand and onto my wrist. "So you and me, we're always going to be together too, no matter what. You're part of my family now." He held my shaking hand in his and looked into my eyes. "You're part of me."

Way off in the distance I could hear the noise of the house: the girls' loud laughter as they gossiped, and the clank and clatter of pots, pans and cutlery in the kitchen sink; my brothers and my dad watching sports on television, alternating cheers and curses. My mother humming Christmas carols, in one of those rare moods where she was actually calm and happy.

But I was oblivious to it all. The house could have fallen down around me and I wouldn't have cared.

I just sat there on the edge of my bed, glancing from Anwar's handsome face and the wide smile on it to my new gift. It was one of those moments, one of those perfectly flawless moments, when everything in the world is right. Or at least it seems like it is, if only for a time. When you know you are truly and deeply loved, and that no matter what happens, nothing on earth is ever going to change it.

If I'd ever doubted that Anwar felt about me the way I felt about him, it was in that precious moment all fear vanished and I knew we were destined to be together forever.

Anwar left shortly after that. He needed to get home and we both knew it. Christmas had been perfect and beautiful and neither of us wanted anything to ruin it. But I'll never forget the feeling that came over me as I watched the red glow of the taillights of his father's car disappear down the prairie highway in the early darkness. How I wanted him to stay. How I wanted to go with him. How I would have loved just to have been with him. Spend the night with him too. I ached for him. I'd never experienced a feeling like that in my life until I'd met him. And I'd never felt it since.

At least, not until I met Frank.

URGE FOR GOING

I WOKE UP GROGGY. Too much on my mind, I guess. So many thoughts running through my head as I thrashed around the sheets trying to fall asleep, flipping and flopping around like a fish out of water.

It was daylight now; the sun was all the way up and I'd slept later than I wanted to. I'd meant to rise early and head out soon after, get a real jump on the day. Funny how life so rarely goes as planned.

There was a knocking somewhere, and someone calling my name. I opened my eyes to see Austin poke his head around the bedroom door. "Can I come in?" he asked.

"Oh. Yeah."

He entered the room, his discomfort apparent. He was dressed as he always was: button-down, cream-coloured shirt and dark denim jeans. "Here," he said, handing me a cup of coffee to cover his unease, his eyes sliding off mine, unsure where to look. "Coral sent this up for you."

Funny how grown men—even brothers—could feel so awkward.

"Thanks," I mumbled, taking the opportunity to compose myself a bit too, sitting up to take a sip of coffee, creamed and sugared to perfection. Coral really did have me all figured out.

"I had a hell of a night," I offered, running a hand ruefully over my sleep-tousled hair and catching a glimpse of Cassie curled up at my feet, unprepared to face the day too.

"That right?" he inquired. "Too much on your mind?"

I nodded as I took another sip. I craved a cigarette but wasn't yet ready to give in. "I gotta get my ass in gear. I want to hit the road soon."

Austin sat down on the edge of the bed. "I envy you sometimes, you know."

"Really?" I asked, surprised.

He nodded. "You can escape all this," he gestured around him. "Long days of drudgery in the fields, worrying about the price of grain, listening to Noel's big mouth all the time."

I was shocked. I'd never heard him talk like this before. I didn't say anything, leaving room for him to say what he'd clearly come here to say.

"He gets on my nerves too," he went on, smoothing the bedspread beneath his callused hand, still not meeting my eyes.

I laughed and he looked up at me.

"How do you put up with it?" I asked.

"I don't know," he smiled ruefully. "You get used to it, I guess. People adjust. You know, I've seen him practically every day of my entire life. I've learned when to listen to him, when to pretend I'm listening, and when to just tune him out altogether."

"Yeah, but doesn't it wear you out? I mean, doesn't it all just get to you sometimes?"

If my brother were any less of a man, I'm sure he would have started crying then. I think he wanted to, he just didn't know how.

He looked away. "Sure. It all gets to me at times. Mom, well, she's become so negative. Moody too."

"Always was," I put in.

"Yup. Always was," he agreed. "And Noel can be such an asshole. Farmin', well, it's a thankless job a lot of the time." He sounded really down then. "Some days...some days I feel like I just want to escape it all. Just pack up and drive away." He stopped talking.

Finally, I spoke. "You know, you're not the only one around here feeling like that."

"What do you mean?"

I hesitated. Should I tell him or not? Should I get involved with my brother's marital affairs or just leave it alone? My sister-in-law had spoken to me in confidence, but…

"Coral," I said, deciding all at once. "I'm pretty sure she feels the same way you do. Maybe the two of you need to talk."

He grew defensive. Curious too. "We *do* talk."

"I don't mean everyday talk," I said, putting the empty coffee cup down on the nightstand, and rubbing my eyes. "I mean *really* talk. Not just about the farm and the kids, I mean. About how you're feeling about things. About how *she's* feeling."

He eyed me, clearly wondering where this was coming from, and stood up. "You know something I don't," he said, pointing at me. "What's going on? What's she been saying?"

I couldn't help it. I laughed. It was so unlike Austin to get worked up over anything. "Now, just calm down," I said, tossing off the covers and pulling on jeans and a sweatshirt. Cass was giving me that look like she needed to go outside. "I don't know much about it, but I did sense a few things."

He paced to the window and back. "And just what did you *sense*?"

I took a deep breath. I wanted to be sure I worded this just right.

"Well, I think she's…a little discouraged these days."

He raised an eyebrow.

"Maybe unfulfilled might be a better word. Bored. Lonely."

"Lonely?!" he exclaimed. "My God, she's always got me or one of the kids around. And when she's not with us, she's with Olive. She's hardly *ever* alone."

I laughed again, amused and frustrated at the same time. "You're not exactly following me," I said. "Put yourself in her shoes. Think about what she's going through right now. Coral's spent her entire adult life being a wife to you and a mother to your kids. And now, with the twins growing up and probably moving away, she feels…"

"She feels *what*?"

"Like she hit a brick wall," I said, throwing my hands out. "Like a huge part of her life is over, and now she doesn't know what to do with the rest of it."

"She's got no reason to feel that way." His hurt and shock were apparent.

I held back a sigh. Older he might've been, but sometimes my brother was *so* naive. "Austin," I said, as I rooted through my duffel bag in search of a pair of socks, "how could you possibly presume to know how she feels? Think about it. Her husband's working all the time, her kids'll soon be gone, and where is she? Out in the middle of friggin' nowhere. Not that there's anything wrong with that, mind you. It's just that sometimes people want a change. Sometimes they *need* it."

He stared at me as I pulled the socks on my feet and grabbed Cassie's leash off the dresser.

"So what do I do?" he asked with concern and bewilderment.

I clipped the leash to Cass's collar and opened the bedroom door. "Talk to her," I whispered, patting his shoulder. "Talk to her."

An hour later we were all gathered around my car, exchanging goodbyes. I had taken Cass for a quick run and sat and sipped coffee with Mom, Austin and Coral afterward. But now it was time to get going, especially if I wanted to see Frank and get back to the city before the day was over.

I was really starting to yearn for more familiar surroundings and had begun to worry about being away from the shop. It was time to sleep in my own bed, bathe in my own tub, eat my own groceries. It had been nearly a week. For a homebody like me, that was enough.

It was quite warm out and we stood around the car talking for several more minutes. I assured my family I wouldn't wait another three years to come see them. I think I meant it when I said it. I really did have great affection for most of them. Some of the talks we'd had in the past few days had been healing and helpful.

My mother broke free of the hug when a thought occurred to her. "Oh," she said. "I was going to send some pickles and jam with you! Would you like some?"

"Sure," I answered. "That'd be great."

"I'm just going to run in and grab you a few jars," she said, starting for the house. "Austin, will you help me carry?"

Austin obediently turned and followed her inside. Coral and I remained standing by the car. She buttoned up her coat, prepared to wait until they returned. It wasn't warm enough to hang outside for long.

"I'm glad you said yes to that," she said. "It makes her feel good. Makes her feel needed when she can do things like that."

"Well, I don't get many homemade preserves in the city," I replied. "It'll be a nice treat."

She smiled her warm, enduring smile. "So, you gonna stop and see Frank on your way back?"

"Don't know," I shrugged, not wanting to make a big deal of it. "Maybe. Haven't really decided. Thought I'd just make up my mind on the way."

"I think you should, Jack. He's pretty great. Men like him don't come along every day."

I laughed. Funny how she was giving me relationship advice just after I'd talked with Austin. I looked back at the house. No sign of Mom and Austin yet. I had a feeling it would be more than a few jars Mom was packing up, but they'd be back any moment. Now was the time. "I had a discussion with Austin this morning."

"You didn't tell him what I told you?" she asked, alarmed.

"Well, not exactly," I hedged. I hadn't outright told him she'd confided in me, after all.

"Then what are you saying?"

"I'm just saying he's got things running through his head too," I told her. "Maybe you two just really need to spend some time together. Some real quality time on your own. Maybe go on a trip; get to know each other again."

She looked toward the house. "Maybe," she said softly.

Mom and Austin came out the front door then, Austin's arms filled with a cardboard box of quart-sealers of pickled cucumbers and pints of jam and marmalade.

I turned to Coral and spoke quietly and quickly. "Look, you're more than welcome to come up to the city and spend as much time with me as you like. But just think about it long and hard."

And with that, Mom and Austin were back at the car. Austin shoved the box in the back alongside my guitar and duffel bag, Cass watching him intently from the front passenger seat. Neither Noel nor Olive would be stopping by to see me off; Noel for obvious reasons, and Olive because she'd said goodbye the night before.

After giving everyone another quick hug, Cassie and I were off. And even though I was looking forward to getting back home, I couldn't help but feel just a little bit torn as I drove away.

GO BACK, JACK

I HADN'T STOOD in front of Anwar's headstone in more than twenty years; not since he'd been buried. It had been difficult enough to do then; I couldn't see why I should do it again. Nevertheless, something had prodded me to turn off the highway and make a quick stop at the cemetery.

Maybe I figured I needed the closure if I were to move forward.

First though, I stared at the pile of dirt flecked with snow under which Dad had been put to rest. I had parked the car on the side of the road beside the small graveyard and walked over to the spot where a proper grave would be completed in the spring, standing silently as I said one last goodbye to my father.

Then, before I had time to reconsider, I had stepped through the snow, the cold of it chilling my feet as it soaked through my loafers.

The words on the concrete stone read *Gone too soon*.

"Sad, isn't it?"

I jumped a little at the soft voice behind me and turned around.

"Sorry, Uncle Jacky, I didn't mean to startle you," my niece said.

"It's okay," I replied, giving her a quick hug. "What on earth are you doing here, Emma? Shouldn't you be in school?"

"I've got a spare period," she replied. "Besides, I needed some down time. Life's been kinda crazy."

I looked at her with affection. Her blond hair had been shoved into a soft pink toque and she wore matching mittens. She'd grown up a lot in the three years I hadn't seen her, physically and in other ways too. There was an elegance and a beauty to her that hadn't been there when she was younger.

"Yeah, life *has* been crazy," I agreed. "I think that's why I'm here. I needed to ponder a few things before the drive back up to Saskatoon."

Emma smiled and nodded toward the grave. "Mom and Aunty Coral told me about your friend Anwar. A couple years ago, they told me what you were to each other and about his…passing. I'm sorry, Uncle Jack. That's—well…it's very sad."

I shuddered. I wasn't sure if it was because of my cold feet or because of what we were discussing.

"It's still pretty chilly out," I said, "even though the sun's out. We should probably get inside." I looked at the empty parking lot and down the roadway. There were no other vehicles but mine. "How did you get here?" I asked. "I don't see a car or anything."

Emma laughed, a girly giggle that brightened my spirits. "Oh, Uncle Jacky, you're too used to the city. I guess you've forgotten. The school's only on the other side of the trees there. We're right on the outskirts of town."

I chuckled. "Guess you're right," I replied.

We stood quietly for a moment, smiling at each other.

"I think I've missed out on a lot not coming down here very often," I remarked. "You and your brother…you've changed so much. You, especially, have become quite the young woman."

She ducked her head, blushing a bit, but I could tell she was pleased I'd noticed.

"Tell me, what are your plans, Emma? You'll be graduating in a little over a year. What will you do then?"

"I don't know exactly," she answered, brushing a flake of snow from her cheek. "My marks are good. I'm thinking I could be a nurse or a teacher. I'd like to make decent money, know what I mean? I want to travel when I get older."

I nodded. "Sounds like you've given it some thought."

"Yeah, I have. I just want to *live*. There has to be more to life than this," she stated, waving her hand around.

I nodded again.

"I'm feeling kind of abandoned," she continued. "Brandon and the twins are all graduating this spring. They're all making plans. I'm gonna be stuck here alone with Mom and Dad for a year."

"Is it that bad?" I wanted to know.

"It's not bad, I guess," she said. "It's just lame."

I smiled again. "Emma," I said. "I think you went and grew up on me."

I started walking back to my car. She followed, keeping up with my large strides.

"How's life with your parents, Em?" I asked. "I mean, is it okay?"

The smile didn't disappear from my niece's face but it changed, fading a little. "Yeah, it's okay," she said. "We're all fine for the most part."

"Noel, I mean…your dad, he treats your mom and you kids okay, doesn't he?" I asked.

"Yeah, he does. Some days he drinks too much. They fight sometimes too, but they always make up. Mom's not afraid to let him know when she's had enough of his bullshit."

I think I flinched a little. It was the first time I'd ever heard any of my nieces swear.

We kept walking. I spotted a headstone that was also familiar to me. "Did you know your grandpa's parents are also buried here?" I asked, pointing at the side-by-side graves a few feet away.

Emma nodded. "Yeah. Mom and Dad have brought us here to show us a few times."

"They were good people, from what I remember of them. They were gentle and kind like your grandpa. So were your grandma's parents, for that matter, though I didn't know them as well."

"Why not?"

"Well, they lived a lot farther away. They were up in Regina. It's amazing my parents ever met, for that matter. If your grandpa hadn't left the farm that one and only summer to go work in the city, their paths wouldn't have crossed."

"I guess it was love. It was meant to be," Emma remarked.

"I guess," I agreed. "Though I'm pretty certain your grandma never wanted to be a farmer's wife. She just kinda fell into it. I'm not certain she ever did become completely comfortable with rural life, with all of its struggles. I think her path might have gone in quite another direction."

"What do you mean?"

"Oh," I said, wondering if I should have started this conversation. "She has a love of history and literature. She told me once she would have liked to have been a historian or an archivist. She showed promise musically too. If she'd kept at it, she could have been quite a pianist."

We got to the car and I watched Emma as she looked back at the snow-filled graveyard.

"You wanna know how I'm getting through Grandpa's death?" she asked.

I pulled the car keys out of my pocket. Cassie sat up, attentive, waiting patiently for me to get back inside. "How?" I asked.

"I just decided no one ever really dies. All they do is go on to a waiting place."

"Oh?"

"Yeah, just a pretty place somewhere. A place to all hang out together until the rest of us get through what we gotta get through here. And then, when we're all done living our lives on earth, we can all be together again."

"That's a nice way of thinking of it," I said, opening the car door.

"Thanks."

I motioned for her to get inside. "Come on, I'll give you a ride back to school."

She laughed. "Uncle Jacky, it's just over there."

"I'll give you a ride anyway."

BREAK FREE

OH, JACKSON, what to do? What to do? The question just kept running through my head as I manoeuvered the Volkswagen down the road. It was why I'd had so much trouble sleeping the night before. Memories, thoughts, choices, possibilities were all running together, eating away at me. What a turbulent week. Lots had happened; lots to absorb, lots to think about. I lit up a smoke. I would be giving up the habit again very shortly, but not today. Certainly not today.

Oh, Frank, you seem like such an incredible man. You really do. But I can't go there with you. That was what had kept me awake the most. I've already had the great love of my life, and although I didn't have him for long, he still held my soul. And so I had remained single. For over twenty years, I had remained single. Oh, sure, I'd had my fun, my rolls in the hay, my one-night stands, my trysts. I *am* human. I'm a healthy, able, gay man after all. Everybody needs a piece of action from time to time. But that's all they'd been and not much more. Didn't ask for much. Didn't get much. And that was how my adult life had gone.

But then, we didn't even have sex, did we, Frank? And yet I'm so drawn to you. And you to me. I was elated when you surprised me by showing up at my father's funeral the other day. I needed a friend, and there you were. I'll never forget that. I love that you think that much of me. That you think me worth driving several hours in less than desirable weather to be there to support me.

To hold my hand when it needed holding. To touch me. To kiss me.

No. No! Stop thinking like this, Jackson. Your mind is made up. You made it up last night, remember? Now do what you have to do and *move on.* Stop and see him briefly to at least talk to him. Tell him face to face, like a real man. You owe him that much. You really do. And then, when you've said your piece, move on. Persevere.

"Yeah, that's what I'll do," I told Cassie, like she could comprehend everything I was mulling over. She looked at me, her tongue hanging out. She was anxious to get back as well. We'd been away from the comforts of home long enough.

Not that my mother's house wasn't comfortable, of course. It was well-maintained, clean and organized. Yet there's something great about sleeping in your own bed, eating your own groceries, sitting on your own toilet. Not having to listen to offhand little remarks that chip away at a guy's self-esteem and self-worth. There's something great about living hundreds of miles away from that. And from other things too.

Noel, for example. What an asshole. I'd always known it. This recent trip south had reminded me of that. What could Olive possibly see in him? There must be something. He must be good in bed.

I reached to turn on the radio. I had been so deep in contemplation that I hadn't even thought to have it on. The DJ was babbling away, complaining about the cold weather and saying he was ready for spring. I listened to him for a bit and then music came on, Nickelback's "This is How You Remind Me." Now *there's* a song—a modern-day classic. I lost myself in the music and the highway and Cassie's soft breathing.

I looked at my watch. Not long to Turn Soil. Not long at all. Frank would meet me on Main Street. But maybe he wouldn't show. Maybe he too would realize that he and I could never really be. Maybe he'd finally come to see how messed up it all was. How messed up *I* was.

Somehow, I doubted it. If there was anything I'd learned about Frank in the short time I'd known him, it was that he was persistent. When he saw something he wanted, he simply pursued it until he got it. He was a hunter, after all.

Perhaps that's what I was to him: the catch of the week, so to speak. Maybe the thrill was in the chase. Maybe if I had sex with him, he'd simply lose all interest.

No, somehow I doubted that too.

If Dad hadn't died, I wouldn't be in this predicament right now. I wouldn't have spent the night in Turn Soil, and Frank and I would never have met. I'd be at work right now. Right this very minute. I'd have just completed all my usual morning rituals. I would have woken in time to give Cass a quick run and scanned the morning paper as I drank my morning coffee. I would have allowed my car to warm up as I quickly showered and shaved. I would have driven down to my shop and stopped quickly at the funky little coffee house next door and purchased a java, a tall one to get me through the day. I would probably have scrubbed the tiles of the store's entryway with that orange-scented cleaner I liked so much.

I would have been completely absorbed in my very manageable life.

That's it. That's what's really bothered me. Up until a few days ago, my life was all very simple. I owned and managed a profitable business and had been somewhat of a loner these past several years.

And now here I was, the one-third owner of a sprawling farm I really didn't know anything about and in complete turmoil over a cowboy living in the middle of nowhere.

How did all this happen?

I looked out the driver's side window and saw a roadside gas station and convenience store. Not in the mood to stop for a sit-down meal, I pulled over and ran in as a strapping young farm-boy poured gasoline into the tank. After a quick bathroom break, I reemerged with a paper bag full of bottled orange juice, a cinnamon bun, some beef jerky treats for Cassie and a bag of peppermints.

I settled back into the little compact car, munching on my impromptu breakfast as I drove. Cassie literally devoured hers before crawling into the backseat to stretch out. The bright sunlight made it seem much more like spring now, so unlike the days before. Much calmer too. I guess that's the comforting thing about stormy weather. I mean, eventually it has to end. It's kind of like a great song. At some point, it's got to reach a crescendo, then come to its completion.

I was enjoying the drive, actually. The weather was great, my belly was full, my spirits were in relatively fine form, and I was with my constant companion. So it was with a real sense of tranquility that I travelled the prairie highway, passing through the countless villages that lined it. And then it was there before I knew it: the big emerald-green sign beside the highway.

Turn Soil: 1 km.

Once again I entertained the idea of just carrying on. But oh, that would be so unfair. Rude and even cruel. He didn't deserve that. Not after everything he'd done for me.

So I slowly headed into town and was turning onto the main drag in a matter of seconds. For one fleeting moment I figured maybe he wouldn't be there. He'd have forgotten or lost all interest.

But the thought vanished quickly enough. The familiar bright blue Silverado was parked right in front of Ming's Café.

And there was certainly no trouble finding him in the restaurant. Besides the owners, who were jabbering away in the open kitchen in the back, he was the only one in the place.

I again found myself drawn to him, by the way he looked in his buckskin jacket and plaid flannel shirt, sipping his coffee, seeming a bit more content than when I'd last seen him. Back home, I guess, back on his own turf, in his own surroundings, with all the things he loved best: his cattle ranch, his animals and his life.

I still remember what he said when I walked toward him. He looked me up and down and his face broke into a dazzling grin as he took a last swig of his coffee. "Man, it's good to see you, Jack."

I sat down across from him. It wasn't long before the same tiny waitress who'd served me supper a few days earlier came over and asked if she could get me anything.

"I'll have a cup of coffee," I said.

She returned with it quickly. I looked around the café as I stirred cream and sugar into the mug. Bright green St. Patrick's Day clovers and cheerful leprechauns had been taped up on the paint-chipped walls since I'd been there. It reminded me that it was nearing the middle of March. I'd been away from my life too long. I felt a sudden desire to down my coffee and get on the road.

"Long drive?" Frank asked.

"Not bad," I replied, taking a sip and quelling my urge to flee.

"I changed my mind," he said softly.

"What?" I asked, nearly choking.

"About taking you out for supper," he said. "I changed my mind. I'm gonna cook you a good meal at home instead. I just came from the grocery store. You like steak? I got a barbecue on my deck. I use it year round. Didn't know what kind of dressing you'd like on your salad, so I bought a few. There's pie too."

"About that," I mumbled sheepishly. "I—I don't know. I'm thinking I should really just be pushing forward. Get home. I need to go to work tomorrow."

He leaned in close. Intimate.

"Oh, Jackson, you've been away this long. Another day ain't gonna make a damn bit of difference. 'Sides, I've been looking forward to this. I'm pretty sure you have too."

We sat and drank our coffee while I thought about what to do.

"All right," I nodded. "You lead the way and I'll follow."

And within a few short minutes, I was steering down a tree-lined gravel road, following Frank home.

POUR SOME SUGAR ON ME

Frank's house was pretty much as I had imagined, full of charm and character, just like him. His tastes were very simple. After meeting his dogs in the yard, Cass was more than happy to follow me inside. Frank assured me his dogs could stay outdoors for a bit. He said they'd be comfortable in their heated dog house and there was no need to make Cassie more agitated than she already was. I'm sure it was a bit traumatic for her, being in completely unfamiliar surroundings and all.

Hell, it was a bit traumatic for *me*.

He made me feel comfortable pretty quickly, though. Frank's kitchen was warm and smelled like wood burning in a cookstove and fresh dill and home baking all at the same time. Half a dozen fresh loaves of bread were cooling on the kitchen counter.

The man never failed to amaze me.

"You bake?" I asked, taking off my shoes in the mud room and stepping onto the polished tiles of the kitchen floor.

"Only once in a while," he replied with a laugh as he hung up his jacket and took off his cowboy boots. "Thought it'd make for a nice supper."

He set his grocery bags down on the kitchen counter. I was impressed by how clean everything was, much like my own kitchen. It was how people were brought up in small towns. Keep the farm running smoothly and the house too.

"Have a seat," he said. "Or maybe I should show you around first?" He chuckled again as he leaned against the counter. "I don't know what the standard procedure is. I don't get a lot of company." For the first time since we'd met, he seemed a little nervous.

"Why don't we have a drink?" I finally suggested, sitting down on one of the antique-looking wooden chairs by the table.

"Great idea," he said. "Rum, right?"

"If you have it," I answered.

And so we sat across the table from each other in the middle of the afternoon. Frank put on a CD and it played softly from the adjacent living room: Jann Arden's cover of Cat Stevens' "Peace Train." Frank sipped a beer and I held my rum and Coke, lifting it to my mouth when things got quiet.

But the awkwardness didn't last long at all. Frank listened intently to my version of what had happened with my mom and brothers over the last couple of days as I took in the sunny kitchen: the bread cooling on the kitchen counter, the ivy spiraling down from the top of the cupboards, and the scenery outside the window over the sink. Light skiffs of snow covered a tiny unpainted barn and chicken coop.

I have to say that a small part of me just wanted to stay there, not just for the day but forever, completely embraced in Frank's strong arms and the sanctuary I felt in the middle of the snow-covered plains.

"I got a few chores to do before the day's over," he said when I finished, swallowing the last of his beer. "Thought I'd do 'em up early. Get 'em over with before supper so we can relax for the evening."

I nodded.

"You can come out there with me, if ya like. Or you can just stay in here and rest. Up to you."

I decided to go with him.

After a quick walk to let her do what she needed to, we left Cass in the house. She wasn't accustomed to being around other animals and neither were his dogs. Frank said at some point we could take the time to help them get acquainted, but by unspoken agreement we decided not to right then. I followed him out to the corral and the barn where I got to meet Cherry and Chestnut and a host of other animals as we fed the barn-cats and milked the cattle. If someone had told me a week ago I'd be doing such things, I probably would have scoffed. But here I was, wearing rubber boots with a bucket in my hand, having a pretty good time with it all.

It was almost dark by the time we got back to the house. Frank removed his outdoor clothes and began washing up in the hand-sink conveniently located in the porch.

"I'm sure you're hungry, Jack," he said as he lathered his wind-burned arms with soap. "Why don't you start prepping us a salad, and I'll get those steaks going?"

I took fresh vegetables out of the fridge, then stood at the counter, rinsing and chopping a head of lettuce, a few carrots, an English cucumber, and Roma tomatoes while Frank slid on a worn pair of slippers and took fresh cuts of meat out to the barbecue. He came back just as I was throwing everything into the big wooden salad bowl he'd left out on the counter.

"Looks good!" he said, pulling out plates and cutlery and setting the table.

"Thanks," I replied. "I don't cook much back in the city. Never seem to have the time."

"Gotta *make* the time," he said as he rummaged through the fridge for butter and whatever other condiments he thought we might need. "'Course, who am I to talk? I don't live your life. I don't know what you go through in a day." He began arranging everything on the table.

"Oh, my life's nothing glamorous," I replied, setting the large bowl on the edge of the table, close to the candle he was now lighting. "Work, eat, sleep, play a little guitar, run Cass. That's about it."

"Thing is," he said as he picked up a plate and went to retrieve the steaks from the outdoor grill, "you gotta have some fun now and again. More to life than just working." He smiled at me to take the sting out of it, then turned to step back out onto the patio.

I grabbed one of the fresh loaves of bread and rooted through the drawers until I found a bread knife. Just slicing into the warm, hard crust made my mouth water.

Frank came back a minute later.

"They're a little rare but they're done," he said.

"I like it rare," I said, meeting his eyes.

He set the plate of meat on the table. The aroma of grilled steak piqued my increasing appetite.

"You know, I *do* have fun once in a while," I said.

"Oh, really?"

"Yeah," I said. "Now and then. Like you said. You're right. A man can only work so hard for so long. And then there comes a time when he needs to cut loose a bit. Take time and relax."

He came toward me. "And how do you know when that time has come?" he asked.

He was a couple of feet away, but I could feel his body heat.

I set the knife down on the counter. "You just know," I whispered, looking him directly in the eye. "You just know."

And then we were in each other's arms, our lips meeting in long, soft kisses. He removed my glasses and then his hands were everywhere; on my chest, on my ass, down my pants.

Before I knew it, he had hoisted me onto the kitchen counter, his muscular arms braced on either side of me. And then he was standing between my legs, his erection pressed against my own throbbing hard-on through our jeans. Cucumber and carrot peels fell from the counter to the floor as we kissed, our hands exploring. And then my T-shirt flew up over my outstretched arms and I took that as an invitation to unbutton his flannel shirt.

Oh, but he smelled good!

It was like I was in a trance then. The next couple of hours seemed almost surreal. Somehow we went from the kitchen to the bedroom, touching all the way, our shadows blending on the hardwood floor.

He lay me down on the patchwork quilt covering his massive feather bed and stood at the foot to remove his clothes in the soft light of the setting sun. We forgot about our meal. We forgot about our nervousness. We forgot about our different worlds.

We simply gave in to our passion.

We didn't have supper for a long, long time.

RUNNING BACK TO SASKATOON

THE DARKNESS OF THE NIGHT was just beginning to break when I awoke the next morning in the stillness of the ranch. Frank was still deeply asleep as I slid out from beneath the covers, threw on my clothes and crept downstairs and into the kitchen, Cassie, as always, right at my heels.

The dirty dishes from the night before waited on the counter, but the kitchen table had been cleared and wiped. We had eventually come down from the seemingly-endless joy of our sexual encounter long enough to hungrily consume the meal, having worked up quite an appetite. A couple of hours of raw sexual exploration has a tendency to make a man ravenous.

Frank had worn only his underwear to the table, while I had clad myself in his flannel shirt, which hung on me just a bit. Frank told me he liked how I looked in it. We talked and laughed and just looked at each other as we ate the steaks, which were cold, and the salad, which was warm, and the bread, which had dried out. The food was all but ruined, but neither of us cared.

I sat at the kitchen table in the dim light of morning, allowing the memories of the night before to wash over me as I basked in the afterglow. It didn't stop me, however, from finding a writing pad on top of the fridge and a pen beside the phone.

Squinting so as to avoid turning on the light, I struggled to compose a quick note to the alluring lone-star who lay sleeping upstairs.

Or so I'd thought.

"What are ya doing, Jack?"

I turned to see him in the wide doorway of the kitchen, completely naked.

"Just writing you a note," I replied softly.

He rubbed sleepy eyes then moved across the kitchen toward the coffeemaker.

"I gotta get going," I added.

"It's early, Jack. It's real early," he said, scooping ground coffee into a filter. "You weren't gonna leave without sayin' goodbye, were ya?"

"That's why I was leaving you a note."

"Are you sure about that?"

He was upset; I could see it in his eyes and in his stance too.

"What do you mean?"

He turned to me, his eyes sparking with unconcealed emotion. I'd never seen him like this. What'd you expect, Jackson? You hardly know the man, after all.

"You're runnin' away," he stated, calmly enough despite the look in his eye, the empty coffee pot still in his hand as if he'd forgotten to fill it with water.

"I've got to get back to my life," I said defensively. "The life I've been away from for far too long now."

"You're running away," he said again, smacking the coffee pot down on the counter. "Just like you always do. Like you ran away from your family all them years ago. Like you run away from everything. Like you run away from *life*."

And with that he vanished up the stairs, leaving Cass and me in stunned silence in the dark kitchen. I ran my hands through my hair, trying to figure out what to do. I could tell it took a lot for Frank to get upset. I also knew I'd pushed his buttons.

Within a minute he was back, dressed in the clothes he'd worn the night before. He hastily buttoned his shirt as he breezed past me to the porch and began hastily pulling on his boots and jacket.

"Where are you going?" I asked quietly.

"There's chores to do," he sputtered. "You ain't the only one who knows how to run away." And with that, he was gone.

I stood at the kitchen sink, watching him stride out to the barn in the soft light of the dawning day, completely knotted up over what to do next. I ran water in the coffee pot and poured it into the coffeemaker, then ran hot water into the sink as well, adding a good dollop of dish soap as I did my damnedest to think it all out. As the coffee brewed and bubbled, I stood there wrist deep in hot soapy water, scrubbing the dishes from the night before.

And when the coffee had completely dripped through the basket and into the pot, I poured two large steaming cups of it, putting cream and sugar into mine and leaving the other black.

That's how Frank liked his coffee.

Wearing a pair of Frank's boots, I carried the two mugs out across the snow-covered yard and into the little barn.

If any man could make his barn cheery and cozy, it was Frank. He stood at a deep wooden storage bin in the far corner of the building, scooping oats into a large bucket. Cherry and Chestnut waited in the two stalls for their morning feed, their deep brown coats thick with fluffy hair.

The routine of it—the warmth of the barn after the chill of snow, the horses' steaming breath, the smell of hay, the sheer day-to-day pleasure of it—touched me somehow.

"I brought you some coffee," I spoke gently.

Frank turned and glared at me, anger still hot in his eyes. "I don't want any right now," he muttered. "I'm busy."

I waited for a few moments. Finally I spoke again. "Why are you so pissed off at me?" I honestly wanted to know.

He poured the oats into the troughs at the front of the stalls. "I ain't pissed off at you, Jack. I'm...disappointed."

"Why?"

"Because of the way you act sometimes. You're a good man, Jack. Hell, I bet you're a *great* man. I really do. I'd like to find out." His voice dropped to a near-whisper. "If you would just let me." He slammed the empty pails down, pulled a bale of hay from the pile beside the oat bin and plunked himself down on it.

Frustration radiated off him in waves.

"I never meant to hurt you," I said quietly.

"Well, you did. You are."

"I…I've got some…baggage."

"I know," he said, and his expression held sympathy along with aggravation. He was calming down some. "I can see it. I can *feel* it."

The barn was really quite warm. Spring must finally be on its way. Yet I felt a bone-deep chill.

"Anwar," he said, and there was a world of pain in his voice.

"What?"

"It's why you were leaving, ain't it? He died, didn't he?"

"Yeah," I said, nearly unable to speak.

Frank moved over on the hay bale, making room for me.

I slowly crossed the barn and sat down beside him. We watched the horses munching away. I handed him his coffee, which I'm sure was nearly cold. But that didn't stop him from accepting it from my shaking hand and taking a sip.

There were several long moments of silence. But finally I spoke.

WELCOME TO MY NIGHTMARE

IT WAS A DAY much like today, cool and crisp; it was still winter, but the thaw was looming close. You could feel it in the air. You could sense it in the townsfolk—people's minds and hearts seemed to brighten like the warm sun beating down on the melting snow and ice.

Anwar and I were on a high too. Things were going our way. We were near the end of our final year of high school, starting to make our plans to venture out into the real world. We had really hit the books hard in recent months. Both of us felt it was important to bring our marks up for the applications we had sent away to the university in Saskatoon. Neither of us had heard back yet, but we were confident we'd be accepted.

We were terribly excited about finally being able to live together and had spent the winter months dreaming of the apartment we'd get in the city. Something close to school and whatever part-time jobs we could get. Classes would not be cheap. We were both very much aware of that.

But nothing—and I mean *nothing*—was gonna stop us from pursuing our dreams.

Anwar and I were also involved in several school activities, which, in addition to studying diligently, was enough to keep any young man occupied.

Being a farm kid, I forever had additional work waiting for me at home after school. So did Anwar. The eldest child of three children who had very busy parents, he too was expected to do chores at home. But this didn't stop us from doing the things we loved. We would often spend our weekends strumming our guitars and going for long nature walks.

The Krochuks had a dugout in the middle of one of their fields, a place kids in the area used as a hangout in both summer and winter. The Krochuks didn't care who visited the tiny man-made lake, and hot summer afternoons often saw countless kids frolicking in and around the pond, laughing, swimming, and splashing around in the water. It was usually a great time. Most of us learned how to swim in that dugout. You didn't have any choice *but* to learn, actually; the water was so deep that you learned to float or you drowned. It was just that simple.

Still, I was never one for the water. I guess I was afraid, much as I hated to admit it. Swimming was always more Austin's and Noel's thing, anyway. Noel especially used to prance around the homemade dock, showing off his muscle-bound, Speedo-clad body to the pubescent girls of the community.

And we gathered there in the winter too, particularly over the Christmas break, but all through the snowy season as well. Guys would meet for hockey games and tournaments. It was a way to burn off some of that pent-up adolescent energy for a few hours. And wherever the guys were, girls would follow, practising figure skating for hours on end, axels and figure-eights, living out their girlhood fantasies of being Dorothy Hamill.

But this particular Sunday afternoon, I knew the dugout would be empty. There was a winter carnival going on in town and the whole community would be there.

Anwar wasn't much for skating. He wasn't much for winter activities at all. He was more of a summer guy. Perhaps his boyhood in India had conditioned him not to enjoy the snowy season. Nevertheless, that late afternoon in March, I persuaded him to join me at the dugout for an hour or two of skating. He wasn't terribly enthused by the idea, but he decided a little fresh air would do him a world of good. Besides, he liked spending time with me.

So off the two of us went in my dad's '56 to the little dugout nestled in the trees just outside of Krochuks' farm, my skates in the back next to an old pair of Austin's for Anwar to wear. I remember how the sense of new beginnings seemed to be in the very air we breathed; spring was coming, and with it a new life for us.

I was the first one to get my skates tied and head out onto the ice, whizzing around the frozen water like I was some kind of super-hero, showing off my skills for my young lover, trying to impress him with various twists and turns.

Anwar followed me onto the ice, his nervousness making him clumsy. I laughed, not to make fun of him, but to make light of it. I was touched by what a trouper he was being, despite the fact that he didn't really like skating. Despite the fact that he wasn't very good at it. Despite the fact that my dad had warned us just before we left the house that the warmer temperatures had begun to melt the ice a bit, here he was, enduring this for me.

Anwar inched across the ice, ankles slanted. He couldn't seem to master the art of being completely upright on his skates. But he *was* beginning to smile a little as he started to relax and just enjoy the warmth of the sun and the time alone together. I circled the pond, zooming around and around, impressed by my own skills encouraging him to catch me. I was at the other end of the ice, absorbed in my acrobatics, when I heard him say my name.

"Jackson."

Anwar *never* called me Jackson. It was always Jack. That struck me as odd. And so did the tone of his voice. I turned.

He seemed fine. Everything seemed fine. I couldn't figure out what could possibly be wrong.

Then I noticed he was looking down. So I looked down too.

And that's when I saw it—an enormous crack in the ice. Actually, there were several cracks. I'll never forget the sound, that hideous sound as the ice split more and more. The look in Anwar's eyes—that terrified expression—is something I'll never forget either, begging, pleading for me to do something. Anything.

But I could think of nothing *to* do. I tried to make my way to him, but all that seemed to do was to make the ice split faster, long thin chunks breaking free as icy water pooled up around the blades of his skates. We stood there for an endless moment, him on the breaking ice and me over an arm's reach away. Neither of us spoke. What was there to say? We were frozen. My eyes held his, taking in his fear, his panic, his anguish. And then he was gone.

I looked down in horror. Anwar flailed around in the dark, freezing water, searching for solid ground. But there was nothing, absolutely nothing, to hold onto. And nothing I could see that could reach him. We were in the middle of a field. There were no fenceposts, no tree branches, nothing to use to pull him out.

My first instinct was to dash forward. But when I did, the hole widened to consume me too. And in that second I knew I could not save him.

So I just stood there. I watched him thrash about the frigid water as he began to freeze and his strength ebbed. It was only a few moments but it seemed to go on forever: the endless agony of seeing someone you love more than anyone else in the world having his life snuffed out before your very eyes, long before it should have been. The agony I've carried with me ever since.

And when the cold and exhaustion had sucked the very last bit of life out from him and I watched his body disappear into the depths, there was no more noise. Just the chickadees in the trees and the sound of my pounding heart echoing in my head.

Until I screamed.

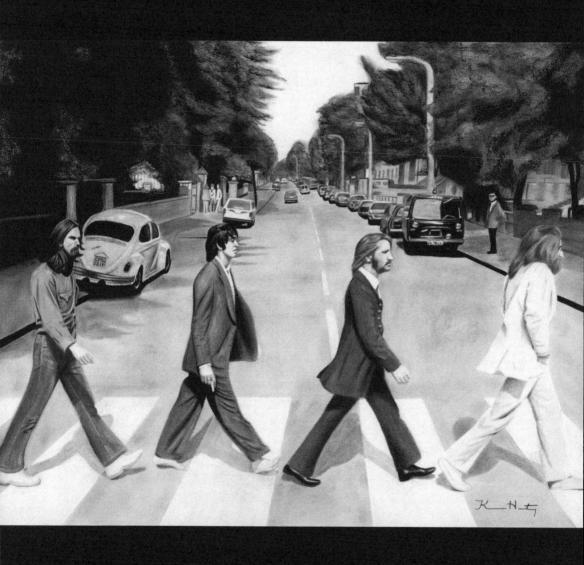

NOWHERE MAN

"I'M SO SORRY," I heard Frank say.

I turned to look at him. I hadn't even noticed that I'd risen from the bale and was standing by the window, leaning against the nearby wall. I'd been so absorbed in the telling of my tale I hadn't even noticed the tears burning my cheeks and making my nose run. It was like I'd gone back in time and relived the whole tragedy.

It was the first time I'd ever told anyone what happened.

Frank was smiling soberly, trying to comfort me. He rose and put a hand on my arm. "Jack," he spoke softly. "That's a terrible story. Something nobody should ever have to live through. Especially a guy as sweet as you." He grabbed my shoulders and stared into my eyes, like he wanted to make certain I was paying attention. "But it wasn't your fault, Jackson. Do you hear me? It wasn't your fault. There was nothing you could have done."

I broke free of his grip. "But don't you see?" I said, pacing back and forth in front of him. "If I hadn't forced him to go skating with me that day…if I hadn't been showing off…!"

"Jackson," he said sternly. "You can't do this. You can't play this 'what if' game. You can 'what if' yourself to death if you allow it."

165

I looked around. Cherry and Chestnut had long since finished their morning oats and were snorting quietly in their stalls, patiently waiting for Frank to take them back out to the corral.

"But it should have been me!" I said, my voice rising. "If someone had to fall in the water, it should have been *me*."

"Jackson, nobody in this world knows what life has in store for them. It's part of the game. We can't go around being afraid to live."

I looked at him. I wanted to take comfort from his words. I wanted to let him make me feel like everything would be all right. But something within me wouldn't.

"It's funny," he said. "They say time heals all wounds, but it ain't really true, is it?"

I shook my head.

"I…think I love you, Jack," he said.

I went back to the bale and sat myself down. "How can you say that?" I asked, running my fingers through my grimy hair. "We met less than a week ago. We barely know each other."

"I know you well enough to know," he replied with a small grin. "When something is really *real* between two people, you just know."

I rubbed my face in my hands, drying the last of the tears. I needed to wash. I needed more coffee. I needed a cigarette.

"Oh, Frank," I said at last. "What do you want me to say? That I'll give up everything to come here and live with you here on your Ponderosa? That we can just shack up here together and live happily ever after?"

"No, I know it all ain't that easy. I know you have a life in the city. A business and other commitments. I ain't naive to that."

"So what are you suggesting?"

"I don't know," he said, lifting his hands in the air, somewhat exasperated. "But I *do* know that if two people love each other enough, they can make it work. They can always make it work."

"You really think so?"

"Maybe I could start driving up to the city. Maybe I could come see you there."

"You'd do that for me?"

He came and sat next to me on the bale. "I'd do just about anything for you," he said, holding my eyes, his gaze soft but steady, until I finally had to look away.

We sat in silence for a couple minutes, not an uncomfortable silence, but more a contemplative one. Finally he stood.

"Okay, I've told you how I feel. You know what I want. But I can't force you to do anything. You have to want to do it yourself." He moved toward the stalls. "So I'll tell you what. I gotta take these two back outside. Then I have a couple more little jobs to do. You do whatever you feel comfortable with. You can either go back up to the house and maybe start makin' us a little breakfast while I finish up—there's bacon in the fridge. Eggs too. Whatever you like." He was leading the horses by their bridles, walking toward the back door of the barn. "Or you can grab your stuff and keep on going, back to the city. You can go back up there and I won't bother you. I won't follow you or try to call you or anything. I'll respect your wishes and leave you alone, if that's what you decide." He turned at the barn door. "Does that sound fair?"

I nodded. I stood for a bit and looked around. And then I began walking. Halfway between the barn and the house, I spotted a burning barrel. I reached into my jacket pocket and grabbed my almost-empty package of cigarettes. I lit the last smoke and took a drag, then tossed it into the barrel along with the rest of the pack.

I walked past Frank's big blue truck, which dwarfed my tiny car. Past the heated doghouse, stopping long enough to give the dogs a few pats as I spoke softly to them. And finally up the steps to the beckoning house.

When I'd left the kitchen to follow Frank outside, it had been dark still, but day had broken over the horizon and a gentle, natural light filled the kitchen. I finished washing the dishes I'd begun to scrub earlier. And after that was done, I went into the bathroom to splash warm water on my tear-stained face and run a comb through my hair.

Up in the bedroom, I straightened the sheets on the bed then smoothed the cover it, memories of the night before coming back to me as I did; the beautiful lovemaking, the passion, the sweet words we'd whispered to each other. I glanced around then for my duffel bag and it occurred to me I hadn't even brought it in from the car. So I started back down the stairs.

The kitchen was clean and bright, nothing remained to be done. If I left now, no trace of my existence would remain. I could just call for Cassie, and she and I could walk out to the car and that would be the end of it. Just like that.

But I went to the kitchen window instead, taking in the patches of melting snow, the small sprigs of green breaking through the earth; taking in the land and the man who worked it as the warm spring day unveiled itself in the brightening sky. Slowly, I reached into the cupboard and began to pull out pots and pans, giving serious thought about what to rustle up for breakfast.

PEACEFUL, EASY FEELING

IT WAS ANOTHER COUPLE OF DAYS before I finally made it back to the city. I'd been gone over a week, which was longer than I'd ever left my home or my business. There was a feeling like returning to Earth the night I turned the key in the lock on my front door and stepped inside. I felt as though something should have been dramatically altered in my absence, but everything in the townhouse condo was just as I'd left it, right down to the Mexican ceramic ashtray full of cigarette butts on the kitchen counter and the toilet seat I'd left up in the bathroom.

I still felt a kind of unaccustomed, displaced calm when I awoke in the cobalt blue of the next morning. Anxious as I'd been all week to get home, I seemed to be in no hurry to do anything that day, drinking coffee in front of *Canada A.M.* and taking Cass for a walk afterward. As our feet sloshed through the slushy sidewalks, I looked in the front windows of the homes we passed and was content to be back in the city with its chaos and calamity.

And when I opened the front door of my shop ten minutes later than the time posted on the door, I laughed at my newfound lack of self-recrimination. This new sense of serenity was as refreshing as the spring manifesting outside with its promise of change.

I was at the front counter going through the same cardboard box of albums I'd abandoned a week earlier when the guys came in. I was trying to decide if we needed yet another copy of The Who's *Magic Bus* on the shelves.

"'Mornin'!" I said.

Ray lifted a hand in a brief wave and walked right past me, the mud from his filthy boots trailing behind him. I chuckled to myself. Had he even noticed I'd been gone?

"How was the trip?" Jim asked, a tinge of concern in his tone.

"It was, uh…interesting."

"Glad to be back?"

"Yeah."

I watched him make his way to the staffroom at the back of the store, removing his coat, scarf and mitts as he did.

"I'd like to talk to you when you got a minute," I said.

He was back a few moments later. "So, what's up?"

A yuppy-ish man meandered into the just store then and I gave Ray a look to suggest he offer the guy a hand. I vaguely heard the yuppy say he was looking for a particular Captain and Tennille song to play at his upcoming wedding before focusing back on Jim.

"I've done some thinking," I told him.

"Yeah?" he asked, adjusting the collar of his black turtleneck. "What about?"

"Oh, lots," I answered, opening the drawer of the cash register, checking the coin, making certain we had enough for the day. "My life, the shop…"

He was suddenly a bit agitated. "What about the shop?"

"We need to make some changes. You know…maybe some fresh paint?"

"Oh. Yeah." He fiddled with a dangling dreadlock.

"Other changes too," I added. "I think I'm gonna need to start taking some more time off."

"That right?"

"Uh huh," I nodded, shutting the cash drawer. "And I started thinkin', maybe it's time to turn the reins over a little, you know."

"Whaddya mean?"

I stared at the *Magic Bus*, admiring the frolicking band members in front of the neon-painted double-decker the album had clearly been named for. Finally I tossed it down on the "in" pile. "I thought maybe we could be partners. I mean…over the last few days I've become a one-third owner of a farm—I'll likely hafta start goin' south a little more often. I mean, not just 'cause of that. There's other reasons too."

Jim let his lips curve in a rare grin as he grabbed a dust cloth from the drawer underneath the cash register and began wiping the counter. "I'm interested," was all he said.

I leaned over the clean glass, catching a glimpse of the wide smile on my own face reflected in its surface.

"Good," I said, with more enthusiasm than I was used to hearing in my voice. "Let's talk."

AUTHOR ACKNOWLEDGMENTS

HEARTFELT APPRECIATION to Kevin Hastings for his amazing artwork, and to the great Jay Semko for his kind words. My continued thanks to the Saskatchewan Writers Guild, the Saskatoon Writers Coop, and the Saskatoon Public Library.

ARTIST ACKNOWLEDGMENTS

My BIGGEST THANK YOU, my largest love, goes out to my family and friends for all the support, encouragement, and help they gave as I went along this path. You helped me become the man I am, the man I was meant to be, the person you see before who has gained confidence to catch his dreams and make them reality. Thanks to Wes for the opportunity to play a part in this new incarnation of *Dead Rock Stars* and to Heather at Your Nickel's Worth Publishing for all the hard work she has put in as we neared publication. Also, to all the people who contributed time and helped this book become the amazing collaboration it is. Gratitude to Jay Semko for the foreword, to Chris Fischer for the cover, and to all the musicians who light our lives with brilliant radiance as they lift our souls through their music—all I did is simply capture their moments! Thanks too to Daniel at Sevenstar Photography and Christina Langman for their photography skills. The biggest thanks is to my wife, Loretta, for her love and support and never giving up as I struggled through darkness to find a place of light, and for pushing me to follow the dream of making art a career. Without you, none of this would be possible. And finally, thanks to my son, Cardinal, who has been my inspiration through his love of life. He is by far the brightest light I have ever encountered.

ABOUT THE AUTHOR

WES FUNK'S FIRST novel, *Dead Rock Stars,* was shortlisted in the Saskatchewan Book Awards, and has also been incorporated into both high school and university curricula.

A love of the prairie lifestyle, a strong belief in diversity, and a passion for music are strong themes in his books. Wes is also the host of the Saskatchewan weekly TV program, *Lit Happens.* Wes lives with his partner and pets in their riverside Saskatoon home.

ABOUT THE ARTIST

KEVIN HASTINGS was drawn to and surrounded by art from a tender age, and has found that pencil, charcoal and paper have consistently been his best method of artistic expression. Using nothing more than the delicate blend of light and shadow across the surface of a page, Kevin converses in the language of art—the stories and emotions that bind people together through appreciation of the visual and aesthetic. Born of Wes Funk's literary talent and Kevin's visual art, a partnership was formed to create *Dead Rock Stars*, the illustrated edition.

Kevin feels exceptionally blessed by the love and support of family and friends, and holds enormous respect, admiration, and gratitude for all the other artists, and patrons of the arts who have made living his dream a reality.